Blame It On The Lattes

Samantha Baca

<u>Sugarplum Falls Series</u>

Blame It On The Mistletoe

Blame It On The Eggnog

Blame It On The Candy Canes

Blame It On The Blizzard

Blame It On The Reindeer

Blame It On The Carols

Blame It On The Lattes

Blame It On The Secret Santa

Cover Design: Richard Baca
Image (s): DepositPhotos

Contents

<u>One</u>
Sam

"Can I help you?" I asked, leaning forward to bend down to see the cutest little girl standing at the counter. I glanced around nervously, wondering where her mother was.

"Can I have a hot chocolate, please?"

"Would you like whipped cream?" I looked down to catch the biggest grin spreading across her rosy cheeks as she nodded yes. Her beautiful blue eyes were a stark contrast to the dark brown locks that framed her cute face.

"How about extra marshmallows?" I offered, loving the way her eyes lit up.

"I think that *might* be a bit of a sugar overload," a soft voice said as I looked up to find my little sister and her best friend standing behind the little girl.

"Come on, Avery, she's technically on winter break. Let her have a little fun," my sister, Cassidy, said.

Avery's eyes drifted to mine, and I felt the same jolt of electricity run through me that I felt the last time I had seen her seven years ago before she moved away to marry the love of her life.

"Alright. But when she's bouncing off the walls tonight, I'm going to remind you that *you* are responsible for her sugar-crazed antics. Between the sugar cookies and now this, she's going to be wired for weeks."

"Well, then, I guess it's a good thing we're having a movie night tonight, isn't it?" Cassidy reached down and planted a kiss on top of the little girl's head.

"Are you in town for a while?" I asked Avery, ignoring the line that was starting to form behind them.

She exchanged a nervous glance with my sister before meeting my gaze again.

"Yeah. Just a few days."

"More like *indefinitely*," my sister corrected as she wrapped an arm around Avery's shoulders. They were the same height and almost the same build, which had always made people joke that they were secretly sisters.

My brows pinched together in confusion. Cassidy and I talked often and were close, so it surprised me that she would be keeping something from me, especially when it came to Avery.

"We don't know how long," Avery said with a heavy sigh.

"Her and Miss Kennedy are staying with me for the time being," Cassidy added. "We are going to spend the day shopping and then heading back to my apartment for pizza and movies!"

"Well, then, how about some lattes to fuel your day?" I offered, knowing better than to push the conversation right now. I'd wait until later and ask Cassidy what was going on.

"Sounds perfect," Cassidy said, playing with Kennedy's hair. "I'll do the salted caramel cold brew, please."

I nodded as I entered her order into the computer, thankful that my assistant manager had opened the other two registers to keep the line moving.

"What can I get for you?" I asked Avery, noticing the way she rubbed her lips together.

"Honestly, I have no idea. I usually do plain, boring coffee. But everything sounds amazing and the aroma in here is messing with my senses."

"The gingerbread latte is really good," Cassidy offered. "It was my grandma's favorite. The peppermint mocha is my go-to when I don't get the cold brew."

"You know what, I'll do the peppermint mocha. That sounds nice and Christmassy."

I entered her drink in and then started working on their order, making sure to give Kennedy more marshmallows than hot chocolate. If they were staying with Cassidy, she could use some extra fun with a wound-up sugar-crazed kid.

"Here you ladies are," I said, handing their drinks to them before grabbing a few candy canes from beneath the counter to give to Kennedy.

"Thank you," Avery said, taking a credit card out of her wallet and sliding it to me.

I shook my head and held my hands in front of me, refusing to take it.

"It's on the house."

"No, Sam. Please, I insist."

"You're good. I promise. Have fun, and make sure Kennedy gets more sugar in her for tonight. Cassidy hasn't had a wild night in a long time," I teased, knowing I would get under her skin.

"Hey, there is nothing wrong with being in my pajamas by six o'clock and enjoying a glass of wine while watching Jeopardy and doing a crossword puzzle," Cassidy objected.

"That's what *old people* do." I raised an eyebrow at her. "You're barely twenty-nine."

"Well, I guess *you* would know," she shot back with a smirk.

"I'm barely thirty-five and couldn't even tell you what channel Jeopardy comes on. I'm too busy being out and about, living my life while I'm still young enough to."

Cassidy rolled her eyes as she turned and faced Avery.

"And by that, he means going and getting shit-faced at his best friend's bar."

"I mean, that does sound kinda fun," Avery said with a giggle, her cheeks blushing the softest shade of pink as she looked up at me from under thick, dark eyelashes. "I can't remember the last time I did that."

I felt a tightness in my chest from the sadness in her voice. There were so many questions I wanted to ask, but now wasn't the time, and the line out the door said it wasn't the place.

Cassidy caught my eye and looked over her shoulder to see what I was looking at.

"We'll get out of your hair. Thanks for the drinks. See

you tomorrow night for dinner." Cassidy grabbed her and Kennedy's drinks she had set on the counter and started toward the door.

"You guys have plans tomorrow night?" Avery questioned, panic in her voice as she stood there, looking between us.

"We do family dinner every Sunday," Cassidy replied with a smile. "And you two are joining us."

"Oh no. We're not trying to impose on anyone while we're here. I told you that we just needed a place to stay for a few days until I figured out the next step."

"And I told you that you're family, and you will stay as long as you need."

They tried to speak softly, but it was still loud enough for me to hear.

Something was going on with Avery, and I hated the worried look on her face. One way or another, I was going to figure out what it was.

Two
Avery

"I really don't think we should be here," I hissed at Cassidy as she held Kennedy's hand while trying to balance a bag of groceries on her hip.

"You're fine, now stop it," she hissed back, giving me a look over her shoulder before turning the knob and opening the front door of her parent's house.

"We're here," she called out.

Warm air that smelled of freshly baked bread greeted us, immediately overwhelming my senses as my mouth watered.

Cassidy set the bag down on a table in the entryway, then helped Kennedy out of her jacket as I hung mine on the rack behind us. I nervously smoothed a hand down the front of my dress, hoping it wasn't obvious how out of place I felt. While I grew up around Cassidy and her family, it had been seven years since I'd been back to Sugarplum Falls, and a lot had changed since then—like me marrying a controlling asshole, having his baby, and then filing for divorce and having to start over.

"Do you need help?" Sam asked as he rounded the corner from the living room.

"We got it, but thank you," Cassidy said, leaning in to hug her brother. "Kennedy is going to help me make macaroni and cheese for dinner tonight."

I smiled at how happy my daughter looked as she bounced excitedly with Cassidy.

"I can't wait. I'm sure it will be delicious," Sam said, smiling down at her.

Cassidy led Kennedy into the living room, and it surprised me how much she already felt at home there. We'd come by yesterday to say hi to Cassidy's parents after she insisted I needed to get over myself when I refused to come for dinner. Amelia and Ron were two of the nicest people I had ever known, and they always made me feel welcome in their house.

 "I brought wine," I blurted out, handing Sam the bottle I had carried inside my purse. "Cassidy said sometimes you guys drink it, but don't feel obligated to indulge because of me."

I shook my head, already irritated with myself for rambling. I tucked a strand of hair behind my ear, trying to give myself something else to focus on other than the way Sam was looking at me.

"Wine is always welcome in this house," he said, accepting the bottle. "We're happy you and Kennedy are joining us for dinner."

"Cassidy didn't give us many options," I joked with a soft laugh. "She threatened to knock me out and carry my lifeless body inside if I didn't agree to come willingly."

"Well, I mean, you did give her a weapon." He held up the wine bottle as evidence.

"True." I laughed, enjoying the way the corners of my mouth felt. It had been so long since I'd smiled, let alone laughed, that it felt foreign to me.

"So, how are things going?" he asked, staying in the entryway.

I shoved my hands into the pockets of my dress and lowered my head.

"They could be better," I admitted. "But soon, I'll be on my feet again, and that's all that matters."

"If there's anything I can do…"

"Thank you. I appreciate that. Right now, I'm just super thankful that Cassidy is offering us a place to stay as we pass through."

"Where are you headed?"

I noticed the same furrow in his brow that I'd seen yesterday.

"I'm not sure yet."

He nodded and rubbed his lips together as if keeping from saying something.

"Well, like my grandpa used to say, life always has a way of sorting itself out."

I smiled the best I could, but it felt like those words were impossible to believe right now. He nodded and led the way into the living room, where I found his parents sitting on the couch, talking with Kennedy.

"Thank you for having us for dinner," I said as they stood to hug me.

"Oh, dear, like I said yesterday, you're always welcome in this house. You never need an invite. Just show up and make yourself at home."

"Thank you." I blinked to try to keep the tears away as I turned to Kennedy, who was tugging on my arm.

"What, sweetie?"

"Can I lay down? I'm tired."

"I thought you were going to help Cassidy make macaroni and cheese?"

"I was, but now I'm tired."

She covered her mouth with her hand and yawned.

"I've got it," Cassidy assured me. "She can go lay down in the guest room if she wants."

"Guest room?" Ron scoffed. "No way. This little princess is staying right here. Get some pillows and blankets, Ma. We're setting up a comfy fort."

"I'm on it!" Amelia said gleefully, shuffling down the hallway.

"They don't have to—"

"Stop," Cassidy said, cutting me off. "They don't have grandbabies yet, so let them enjoy this. If Kennedy wants to rest, let her. I've got dinner. Just relax and take a break for once. You don't have to do all of this on your own anymore, Avery."

The tears prickled my eyes again, making my nose burn as I tried to force them away.

A few minutes later, the couch bed was pulled out, piles of blankets and pillows were added to it, and somewhere inside the mess was my happy little girl.

I sat at the kitchen table, watching everyone as I thought about how different their lives were from mine. I was never close to my family growing up as a single child to two parents who were married to their jobs. I cherished the time I spent at Cassidy's house because her family always made me feel like I was one of them. But along the way, I'd forgotten what that felt like.

I'd gotten married seven years ago and moved to North Carolina, where Grant and his family were from. When we first got together, I was impressed by his drive and ambition. I trusted that he worked hard so he could build us the life I always wanted. When I got pregnant with Kennedy two years later, everything slowly started to change.

Instead of Grant spending more time at home with us, he spent more time in the office. He was constantly traveling, and I never bothered to question why all of his extra dedication to his job never seemed to improve our quality of life. We went from being a single-income family and me being a stay-at-home mom taking care of Kennedy to us needing two incomes and me working sixty hours a week sometimes just to make ends meet.

It wasn't until I accidentally opened his bank statement that I found out where all of the money was going. He had not only been cheating on me for the past two years—hence the bogus work travel, he'd also been buying said mistress everything her heart desired while our family suffered.

There were charges from some of the most elegant boutiques that I'd only ever dreamed of visiting to several large cash advances that never made their way to our bank account. Once I found out, I immediately contacted a lawyer and filed for divorce. Unfortunately, the divorce was messy and took over a year to finalize, which resulted in Grant getting to keep everything we'd built together over the past seven years. But none of that mattered because I got sole custody of Kennedy. I didn't ask for anything else because none of it meant anything to me. Everything we had was built on lies, and I wanted a fresh start. I might not have had a penny to my name, but I had the only thing in life that made it worth living.

"Stop it," Cassidy scolded, eyeing me from across the kitchen as she worked on dinner.

"Stop what?" I asked, getting up from the table and joining her at the island that separated the kitchen space from the living room.

"I can see you over there thinking about him. Stop it. It's going to give you wrinkles from all the frowning you're doing," she teased with a wink.

"It's not that easy," I admitted, smiling even though it felt forced.

"Do you still love him?" she asked cautiously.

"What? God, no." I pulled my head back and scrunched my face in disgust. A few months ago, my answer would have been different. But after finding out everything he had been doing to tear our family apart, I couldn't find the love I used to feel for him anymore.

"Then you have to try to let it go. Don't let him take another ounce of your happiness."

"It's not my happiness he took. It was the money I'd busted my ass working for and stupidly put into our joint savings account."

"I know. But that's done and over. Now you forget about it and we will figure out your next step."

"How am I supposed to take the next step when I feel like I can barely even stand on two feet?"

"You don't. You stop. You rest. You give yourself some grace because you are an amazing mother, and you *will* get back on your feet. Until then, you lean on your family to help you guys. There's nothing wrong with needing some help, Avery."

I turned and tried to blink away the tears, but her arms wrapped around me before I could stop them. I cried quietly while my best friend held me, promising me everything would be okay.

14

Three
Sam

"The chicken is delicious," I said, wiping my mouth with a napkin.

"Thank you," Cassidy said, smiling.

While we did Sunday dinner at my parent's house every week, we took turns on who cooked it. That way, it didn't always fall on the same person to do all of the cooking.

"Do you like the macaroni?" Cassidy asked Kennedy, who had a giant spoonful ready to shove into her mouth.

"It's cheesy," she answered with a giant grin.

"That's because I added extra cheese." Cassidy smiled and wiggled her eyebrows playfully as Kennedy took a bite.

"You're going to spoil her," Avery teased with a smile and shake of her head.

"That's what aunts are supposed to do."

"Does that mean Sam's my uncle?" Kennedy asked around a mouthful of macaroni.

I felt Avery's eyes on me as she stalled in answering her daughter. We hadn't talked about any of this, and it wasn't like I had known Kennedy until yesterday. Her relationship with Cassidy was a lot different due to how much time they'd spent together and how often Cassidy had gone to North Carolina to visit after Kennedy was born.

"You know what I heard?" Cassidy said, clearly changing the subject. "I heard that Santa's reindeer are coming for the Frosty Fest this year!"

"What's a flosty flest?" Kennedy asked, still not having finished her bite.

"Don't talk with your mouth full," Avery scolded gently, placing her hand on Kennedy's arm to get her attention. "And please take smaller bites. I don't want you to choke."

"But thits so good," Kennedy objected, continuing to talk with her mouth full.

"It'll still be just as good with smaller bites."

"Frosty Fest is an annual event that we do in Sugarplum Falls," Cassidy answered, looking at Kennedy and avoiding Avery's gaze that was on her. "There's always a lot of fun shopping, but the best part is the parade in the morning to kick it off. Santa and Mrs. Claus come, and they bring the reindeer! After the parade, you can go visit the reindeer and feed them carrots!"

Kennedy's eyes widened as she looked from Cassidy to Avery.

"Can we go?" she asked excitedly, finally having finished her bite.

"When is it?" Avery asked nicely, though I could see the daggers she was shooting into my sister's head.

"Two weeks." Cassidy pinned Avery with an equally threatening look as she lifted her fork to her lips and took a bite of chicken.

"I don't know if we'll still be here," Avery said gently to Kennedy, her eyes softening as disappointment washed over her face.

"Okay."

I could feel the tension mounting on Avery's shoulders from where I was sitting, and though I didn't know the whole situation, I wasn't happy with my sister for what she just did. Once dinner was over, I sent Avery and Kennedy to the living room with my parents to watch a movie while Cassidy and I cleaned up.

"What the hell was that shit you just pulled on Avery?" I bit out angrily as I filled the sink with hot water.

"What are you talking about?" she asked while setting down a stack of plates from dinner.

"Why would you tell Kennedy about Frosty Fest without checking with Avery first? Now you've gone and disappointed Kennedy while also making Avery feel like shit for not being able to promise her daughter they can go."

"Look, I know you mean well, but you don't know anything about what's going on with Avery and Kennedy."

"You're right. I don't. But I know a lot about family and friendships, Cassidy, and you don't do shit like that to someone you love."

She sighed heavily, pushing the air forcefully out of pursed lips.

"I don't want them to leave, okay?"

I pulled my head back in surprise, not believing what she just said.

"This isn't about *you*. It doesn't matter what *you* want. You don't get to make things harder for Avery just because you don't want them to leave."

"I'm not trying to make things harder for them. I'm trying to help out the best I can. She doesn't have anything right now, Sam. Not a penny to her name. Her dumb-ass ex took it all when she filed for divorce. She's having to start over, and the only thing she got from him was a beautiful daughter who she loves with all of her heart. If I can keep them in Sugarplum Falls, then I can help them. I can give them a safe place to live where Avery doesn't have to worry about how to pay the rent. It's less than three weeks until Christmas, and she can't even afford gifts for her daughter. How is *Santa* supposed to come, Sam?"

She turned away and wiped the tears from her eyes, not wanting anyone in the living room to see. Thankfully, the TV was up loud enough that no one could hear what we were talking about.

"Shit," I muttered, shoving a hand through my hair. "I didn't know it was that bad."

"She's my best friend. She's like the sister I never had. I love her and Kennedy so much that it kills me that this is what they're going through right now. So yeah, it was a shitty thing to do by getting Kennedy excited about Frosty Fest, but what else am I supposed to do? How is she supposed to experience the magic of Christmas if we don't help? They're literally in the most Christmas-obsessed town, and yet they haven't experienced any of the joy it brings. You can't fault me for wanting to give that to them."

"We'll figure it out," I assured her, wrapping my arm around her shoulders.

"You don't have to do anything, Sam."

"It's family, Cassidy. We rally around our family and help them. You know that."

Four
Avery

By the time the movie ended, Kennedy was yawning and getting a little too comfortable on the couch bed Cassidy's parents had made for her. Thankfully their living room was large, so there were two other couches the rest of us could sit on without having to be huddled together on hers.

"You ready to go, sugar pie?" I asked, making eye contact with her before her eyes could flutter closed again.

"Do we have to?"

"Yes, baby. We need to get going so Amelia and Ron can get some rest, too."

"I don't want to go," she whined, digging herself deeper into the couch.

I took a slow, deep breath, trying not to let myself get worked up. Kennedy was a sweet girl, but she was also a typical five-year-old, which meant her moods could give anyone whiplash, especially when she was tired.

"Crap," Sam said from the other couch, staring down at his phone as he rubbed his hand down the scruff on his face.

"What's wrong?" Cassidy asked.

"My new barista just quit on me. His family is going out of

town for the holidays, so now I'm shorthanded and don't have time to look for someone else."

"Shit. That sucks," Cassidy replied before shooting me a grimaced look. "Sorry."

"She's heard worse," I replied with a laugh. "And she's already asleep."

Great. Just Great.

"What hours do you need someone?" Amelia asked. "I can see if anyone from the community center might be able to help out."

Sam shook his head as his fingers flew across his phone.

"Thanks, Mom. I don't want to be ungrateful, but I need someone who can handle a fast-paced environment and juggle multiple things at one time. Someone who isn't bothered by loud noise or chaos. I don't want to have to shout the orders over and over while waiting for hearing aids to properly adjust."

"Someone like Avery," Cassidy suggested, nudging me with her elbow.

I glared at her for a split second before looking over to find Sam's eyes on me.

"I don't know anything about coffee," I admitted sheepishly as I tried to blend in with the couch.

"You don't have to," Cassidy said, continuing to interject herself. "Sam can teach you the basics. You're a quick learner. Plus, you're an elementary school teacher—you're used to the chaos and loud noise. Not only that, you're fully capable of juggling lots of things at one time. Perks of being a mom *and* a schoolteacher."

"Are you interested?" Sam asked, his eyes wide and full of hope.

I shifted again, not sure if I had ever been more uncomfortable in my life.

"I would hate to let you down," I replied with a nervous laugh.

"Why do you think you would?" he questioned, setting his phone down and giving me his full attention.

"I don't know." I shrugged and made a weird face I would later regret. "What if I can't learn how to make the drinks?"

"Then I'll make them, and you can work the register."

"What if something happens and I don't have someone to watch Kennedy? We don't even live here, and I don't have a babysitter lined up."

"We'll watch her," Amelia and Ron answered at the same time while Cassidy grinned like a fool.

"I appreciate that. I really do. But you guys have your own lives. What about when you have doctor's appointments or need to run errands?"

"Then I'll watch her," Cassidy said, pinning me with another look.

"But—"

"Avery, I think it's clear that you have support with someone watching Kennedy. And worst-case scenario, if you don't have someone to watch her, then you bring her with you to work and I keep an eye on the marshmallow inventory," Sam said with a wink.

I shook my head, not sure what to think about all of this.

"I don't know how long I'm in town for."

"I need immediate help, Avery, and as far as I can see, you're in town for a little while. Why don't we help each other? You keep me from having to scour the high school to see if there are any eligible seniors who *might* want a job, and I give you something to do with your day so you're not stuck with Cassidy 24/7. It's a win/win."

"Ugh, rude." Cassidy frowned, giving her brother a dirty look.

I pulled in a deep breath and slowly released it. It was like the universe was giving me what I had been praying endlessly over: a chance to give Kennedy the best Christmas ever. Not knowing how I would afford gifts had been stressful enough to give me an ulcer. This would allow me to do that for her and keep the magic alive by having something for her from Santa on Christmas morning.

"Okay. I'll do it. When do you want me to start?"

"How about tomorrow? 6 am sharp."

Thankfully, I was an early riser, so that wasn't a problem for me.

"I'll be there." I turned to Cassidy, ready to ask for my first favor by having her watch Kennedy.

"She's already asleep, so why don't you leave her here, and I'll stay over too. You can go back to my place and not have to worry about anything other than getting up and starting your new job in the morning."

"You don't have to do that," I said, my voice nearly breaking again.

"We want to," Cassidy assured me as her parents nodded from the other couch. "This is what family does."

25

Five
Sam

Avery showed up at 5:45, ready to start, which was a surprise to me. I was used to grumpy teenagers who looked like they had just thrown themselves out of bed and zombie walked in the door *after* the time they were supposed to start working. But not Avery. She was wide awake and looking more radiant than ever. Her long dark brown hair was pulled into a messy ponytail on her head, and her eyes sparkled with the natural-looking makeup she wore.

"Good morning," I said as she came through the door.

"Good morning. Sorry I'm a few minutes early. My biggest pet peeve is people being late, so I make up for that by constantly being too early."

"That's never a problem," I assured her with a smile. "I already got you set up in the system, so I'll show you how to clock in and out."

She followed me to one of the computers in the back by my office and sat down while I instructed her on what to do. She was a quick learner, which I knew she would be. Within the first hour, I had already shown her the basics of how to use the coffee machines, though I expected she would need more training since they could be tricky.

The morning started slowly, allowing me time to train her

on the cash register before having her take over. It was a relief to know that she was able to jump in and take the lead on what I needed her to do. I didn't have to tell her things over and over, nor did I have to remind her to smile and be friendly to the customers. Avery was a natural and I could picture her in the classroom with a room full of kids who adored her.

By the time our morning rush picked up, I was in my office getting a few things taken care of while Avery worked with Piper, the assistant manager.

"Hey, I'm sorry to bug you," Avery said, peeking her head around the door of my office. "Piper is busy fixing the espresso machine, and the others are busy, too. I have someone asking for a black eye, and I don't know if that's some sort of fancy coffee drink or if I should punch him. The way he's smiling, I feel like maybe it's a trick?"

"Punch him," I said, leaning back in my chair and grinning.

Her eyes widened before her brows pulled together in confusion.

"Ummm… Okay?"

"Tell him we're all out and that he can have a vanilla latte."

She nodded, still looking confused as she walked away.

I gathered my phone from the desk and tucked it into my pocket right as she returned.

I raised my eyebrows, curious what she was going to say.

"He said he's going to come back here and beat your ass if you don't stop it with your shit this morning."

I chuckled and shrugged, leading her back to the front with my hand on her lower back, making sure to keep it friendly and not crossing any lines.

"Do people seriously get this angry over coffee?" she whispered, turning her head so he couldn't see what she was saying as we approached the register.

"Na. This guy is just constantly grumpy. A big ol' ass, if you ask me," I said, grinning at Aiden.

"I seriously don't have time for your shit this morning," he mumbled under his breath, but the humor in his eyes said otherwise.

"You always have time for my shit."

"Should I go help someone else?" Avery asked, looking between us.

"Ignore both of them," Piper said from behind us as she smacked the bottom of the espresso machine. It was usually the trick to get it working, but I knew it was only a temporary fix until I had to buy a new one. "They're both being worse than this stupid machine."

"I'll look at getting a new one soon," I told her, knowing it didn't help that we had a handful of people impatiently waiting for their drinks.

"Today would be great, but since that's not happening, we're just going to have to make do." Piper gave it another smack and then let her head fall back with relief as it sputtered and came to life. "Go let everyone in line know that the espresso machine is slow this morning. We're going to separate the line and move those who would like a latte to the register closest to the window, and those who want straight coffee or pastries can go to the middle line so we can get them in and out quickly. Everyone already in line can get a free muffin of their choice for the wait this morning."

The two employees she was working with rushed through the line, letting everyone know.

"Do I get a free muffin since you're being ridiculous this morning?" Aiden asked as people started shifting around to the appropriate lines.

Avery looked nervously from me to him, unsure what to do.

"Stop being a crybaby. I'll get you your damn coffee," I teased, rolling my eyes before turning my attention to Avery. "It's a black coffee with two shots of espresso. Piper can help you with the other espresso machine if you need it."

"I think I got it, but thank you. I'll be sure to ask her if I need help."

I nodded and smiled at her while feeling Aiden's curious gaze locked on me. Once Avery was out of earshot, he started.

"So, new hire?"

"That's Avery, Cassidy's best friend," I explained with a shrug. "She's in town for a little while, and I needed the help after Jonathan quit last night."

"You knew that was going to happen from the day he started. Kid took a three-hour lunch after coming in late and then asked to leave early."

"True. I guess I just expected things to be somewhat better since he seemed to be making more of an effort lately."

"So, is she a barista somewhere else? Or is she just a quick learner?" he asked, nodding to the espresso machine she already seemed to have mastered.

"She's actually a teacher."

Aiden's eyebrows rose to the top of his forehead as a shit-eating grin spread across his face. I already knew where this was going, which instantly turned my cheeks red with embarrassment.

"Whatever you're thinking—stop. It's not like that. She's my little sister's best friend. She needed a job, and I needed help. It was a win-win situation."

Aiden shook his head and sighed heavily.

"What? What's with the sigh?" I asked, trying not to let the irritation mount.

"Nothing."

"Bullshit. Just spit it out."

I glanced over my shoulder to see Avery asking Piper a question.

"I just think it's funny that you hired her on the spot when she doesn't have any experience, then get super defensive when you talk about her."

"Because you were insinuating that there would be something happening, and there's not."

"I never insinuated shit. I reacted to you saying she was a teacher because I remember you obsessing over your future wife when you were a kid and always saying she would be a teacher because she would love kids and have seven of yours."

"That was a long time ago. I'm not ten anymore."

"No. But the way you blush when you talk about how nothing is happening between the two of you tells me that you *wish* something would happen between the two of you."

He finished just before Avery came back, wearing a smile and holding his drink proudly.

"Here you go, one large black eye. Can we get you anything else?"

"Just the coffee. Thank you." Aiden gave me a look before pulling out his debit card and handing it to her.

"Go ahead and toss a muffin in for him on the house," I said, grinding my jaw in frustration. "He's going to need something to balance out that caffeine overload."

I didn't wait to hear if he objected as I made my way back to my office and tried to forget what Aiden had said. Even if I was interested in Avery, it wasn't like I could do anything about it.

<u>Six</u>
Avery

The first week working for Sam flew by and I hadn't realized just how tired I was until the weekend rolled around and I didn't want to get out of bed. I was so used to sleeping on the comfortable pillow top mattress Grant had insisted on buying when I got pregnant with Kennedy that my body was actively objecting to every uncomfortable bed I'd slept on since.

It had been a little over two weeks since I'd packed my SUV and left with Kennedy, not knowing where to go and showing up unexpectedly on Cassidy's doorstep. Her apartment was small, but she made room for us, giving Kennedy the guest bedroom that only had a twin-sized bed while I took the couch.

We knew it was a temporary solution until I could get on my feet again, but I was finding that to be harder than I could have imagined. I made good money working for Sam, but I had to decide whether I wanted to use that money to try to get us our own place or if I wanted to use it for Christmas gifts for Kennedy. It was a no-brainer, but I still felt terrible about imposing on Cassidy.

I sat at the small kitchen table and sipped my coffee while Cassidy took a shower. We were supposed to go shopping today, but I had a hard time being excited about it, knowing that I wouldn't be able to buy anything until I got my first check from Sam next week. It was hard taking a five-year-old to the store and telling them they couldn't have anything. If that didn't crush your heart, nothing would.

"Good morning," Cassidy said, drying her hair with a towel.

"Morning."

"You okay?"

"Yeah, just tired." I didn't want to complain about how sore my body was or that I was so uncomfortable that I hadn't slept well in the week we'd been staying with her. She went out of her way to accommodate us; I wasn't about to be ungrateful.

"Maybe some coffee and then shopping?"

Before I could answer, Kennedy came in, rubbing her eyes.

"Good morning, sweetheart," I said, reaching for her as she held her arms out to me.

I picked her up and then frowned when I felt her pajamas were soaking wet.

"Did you have an accident, baby girl?"

"No," she said, leaning her head against my shoulder as she nuzzled close to me. I immediately felt the heat coming from her body and lifted my hand to her forehead.

"What's wrong?" Cassidy asked, standing beside us with concern etched on her face.

"She's burning up, and her clothes are wet." I pulled her

away slightly so I could get a good look at her. Her eyes were glossy, and her cheeks flushed. "Do you have a thermometer?"

"Yeah. Let me go grab it real quick."

"Thanks. And I'm sorry, I think she had an accident. It happens sometimes when she's sick."

"I didn't have an accident," Kennedy objected, clinging tighter to me. "There was water dripping on me, and it woke me up."

Cassidy and I both frowned, about to ask what she meant when we heard a loud noise. I jumped up with Kennedy still in my arms as we rushed to the bedroom where she had been sleeping.

A giant hole opened in the ceiling as water poured inside.

"Oh my God!" Cassidy shrieked, holding her hands in front of Kennedy to keep her from getting splashed by the water that was pouring in. "Get her out of here! We need to get out of the apartment before the rest of the ceiling collapses."

I nodded and hurried out of the room, stopping to grab my phone from the table before heading outside. Cassidy had her phone pressed to her ear as we stood in the parking lot, staring in disbelief as we heard another loud crashing noise.

I walked over to my SUV and sat on the curb in front of it, hating that I didn't have my keys so I could get Kennedy inside. She was sick, and it was freezing outside, which wasn't the best combination right now. I still had pajamas on with nothing to offer her to keep her warm except my body heat.

"Here honey, take this," an older woman said, coming across the parking lot and handing me a blanket. I had seen her a handful of times and knew she lived next door to Cassidy.

"Thank you. I appreciate it." I wrapped the blanket around Kennedy and held her close to me as I rocked her back to sleep.

Before I knew it, fire trucks and paramedics filled the parking lot as people rushed about. Cassidy came and joined me on the sidewalk, looking completely lost.

"Did they say what happened?"

She nodded, her face pale.

"The older woman who lived above me had been running a bath but had a medical episode and died. They said it looked like it had been a few days since it happened and that the leak likely started small, but the ongoing water pressure from the tub continuing to fill caused the entire ceiling to collapse."

"Oh my God," I whispered, covering my mouth with my hands while trying to keep from waking Kennedy up.

"It's a good thing she got up when she did," Cassidy said, shaking her head. "I can't even—"

"Don't," I interrupted, not able to hear her finish her sentence.

We sat there in silence for a few minutes while we watched the paramedics bring out a gurney covered with a sheet. My heart broke for the poor woman, wondering if her fate would have been different had she had someone there with her who could have called for help when it happened.

"Hey, are you guys alright?" Sam said, startling me as he stood in front of us.

"Yeah. We're fine," Cassidy answered with a shaky breath. "They said it's going to be a while before I can go back since they have to deal with the water damage and fix the ceiling. I talked with Mom and Dad, and they said we can stay with them until then."

She smiled at me and gave my arm a soft squeeze.

"I can't do that," I objected, already knowing how crowded it would be. Cassidy and Sam had grown up in that house, but they had since converted his bedroom into a craft room for Amelia. Cassidy's room was big enough for her, but it wouldn't fit the three of us easily, which meant Kennedy and I would have to sleep on the couch with nowhere to store our stuff.

"It's not a problem," Cassidy insisted. "You and Kennedy can take my room. I have a blow-up mattress we can put in there. I'll sleep on the couch. I don't mind."

"I'm not doing that, but thank you. I'll check into a hotel for a few days until we figure out the next step."

"I hate to break it to you, but there's nothing available. Everything was booked months ago. You'd be lucky to get a last-minute cancellation with it being a week until Frosty Fest." Cassidy smiled sympathetically, but it did nothing to dull the burning pit of fire I now had in my stomach.

This wasn't an ideal situation, but I would figure something out and make it work.

I rubbed my lips together as I tried to think about other options. Just because the hotels in Sugarplum Falls were booked didn't mean that the neighboring towns would be booked as well. It would be a further commute to work, but I could figure it out.

"You and Kennedy will stay with me," Sam said, bringing my and Cassidy's attention to him.

"I'm sorry. What?"

"You and Kennedy will stay with me." He nodded as if this decision was final.

"Sam, no. You've done enough for us already by giving me a job. I couldn't ask—"

"You didn't. I'm offering it to you, Avery." He rocked back on his heels and shoved his hands in his pockets as a gust of cold air whipped past us. "Technically, I'm telling you that's what's happening. Cassidy will stay with my parents, and you and Kennedy will stay with me. I have two guestrooms that I don't use."

I opened my mouth and then snapped it shut, unsure of what to say.

While I didn't want to take advantage of Sam's kindness, I honestly wasn't in any position to be picky right now. It wasn't just me and my pride I had to worry about. It was my baby girl, who was sick and needed a safe place to stay.

"I'll pay you rent," I offered, feeling the knot in my stomach get tighter as I thought about how I didn't have the money to do that.

"You will not."

My eyes widened, not sure how to handle *bossy Sam.*

"I called Aiden. He's on his way with his truck. We'll load up what we can and get you guys settled in. Here are my keys. Why don't you get Kennedy situated in my truck so she doesn't freeze out here? Cassidy can help get your stuff."

"Okay," I said, not having it in me to fight. I looked around for something to hold on to so I could get up with Kennedy wrapped around me, but before I could, Sam reached out and gently took her from me before extending his hand to help me.

"It's the black one over there," he said, nodding to it. "Go ahead and let her sleep for now, and then we'll worry about waking her up and putting her in her booster seat once we're ready to go."

"Thank you. You have no idea how much I appreciate this."

He smiled a smile that could warm even the coldest days while I forced my heart not to get used to it.

Seven

Sam

"How is she feeling?" I asked Avery as she sat curled up on my couch with Kennedy sleeping on her lap.

"She's still running a fever, but it's not as high as it was. Thank you again for everything you've done for us today."

"It's my pleasure." I sat down in the chair across from her and tried to ignore the way my heart danced every time I saw her. "I grabbed stuff to make her chicken noodle soup while I was at the store. I also grabbed some frozen pizzas and stuff to make dinner this week. Is there anything that sounds good to you?"

"Sam, you don't have to keep spoiling us like this. You've already given us a place to stay and went to the store to get medicine for her. You've done more than enough. If anything, *I'm* the one who should be making dinner for *you*."

"You don't need to do that, Avery."

"Trust me, it's the least I'm able to do to show the gratitude I feel."

I could hear the sadness and frustration in her voice, but decided to let it go. I didn't want to make her feel worse when I knew how much she was already struggling with everything. My goal was to make things easier for her without her feeling like she owed me.

"So, maybe a pizza tonight? That way, if Kennedy doesn't feel like soup, there's at least something else she might eat."

"That sounds fantastic. Thank you."

I smiled and got up to fix dinner. It had been a while since I'd made chicken noodle soup from scratch, but I was pleased when everything came back to me easily. For a moment, I was transported back in time to my grandmother's kitchen as she taught me to make it.

I popped a frozen cheese pizza into the oven and set the timer while I stirred the noodles, waiting for them to get to the perfect softness.

"Is that chicken noodle soup?" a soft voice asked, pulling the corners of my lips up.

I turned around and found Kennedy in the kitchen, climbing onto one of the chairs at the island as Avery helped her.

"It is. I made it myself. Would you like some?"

"Yes, please." Her little nose was red, and her cheeks still flushed, but she looked better than she had when I found them sitting on the curb this morning. It had shattered my heart to see her curled up against Avery, trying to stay warm in the storm that was moving in, but I had been incredibly thankful that she had gotten out of the room before the ceiling collapsed.

I poured her a bowl and set it in front of her, thankful that she didn't rush to try to eat it and accidentally burn herself. Avery lifted a spoonful out and blew on it several times before offering it to Kennedy.

It warmed my heart to see the way her eyes lit up at the first taste. I knew children could be picky eaters, and I didn't want to let Kennedy down if I failed at making chicken noodle soup. The way she begged her mom for more had me feeling over the moon as I pulled the pizza out of the oven and set it on a trivet.

"Is that pizza?" Kennedy asked, her eyes wide as saucers.

"It is. I wasn't sure what your tummy might feel like for dinner, so I made a few options."

"Can I have pizza, too?" she asked Avery, turning to look at her.

"I don't see why not. Let's get some more soup in you while we wait for the pizza to cool down," Avery said, brushing her thumb against Kennedy's lip as she gave her another bite.

"Can we have a movie night again?" Kennedy asked with more energy than I'd seen her with all day.

"I think it's better if you rest," Avery replied at the same time I blurted out, "sure."

I didn't want to overstep with Kennedy and upset Avery, but at the same time, I wanted both of them to feel comfortable in my house.

"Sorry," I apologized and turned to grab some paper plates from the pantry.

"No, it's fine. As long as you're up for it, we can stay up

and watch a movie. But you do need some rest since you're sick."

"Okay, momma."

I cut the pizza into slices and grinned like a lovesick fool.

Eight
Avery

I was never leaving Sam's house.

Correction—I was never leaving his guest room.

Not only were the rooms big compared to the guestroom at Cassidy's apartment but they were also joined by a Jack and Jill bathroom, which allowed me to keep an eye on Kennedy with the doors open. And if that wasn't enough, Sam had gone out and purchased a baby monitor with a camera so I could keep an eye on her while she was sick.

We had stayed up to watch *The Grinch*, but she fell asleep during the last twenty minutes of it. Sam graciously carried her to bed for me, and I almost cried when I saw the handful of new stuffed animals he had added when I wasn't looking.

He had gone above and beyond for us without anyone asking. It wasn't just him giving us a safe place to stay; it was him making sure we had all of the little extras that would make us feel special and comfortable.

When I got to my room, I found five different pillows waiting on the bed with a note about how he didn't know what level of firmness I liked, so he bought them all. I was pretty sure he was certifiably crazy for doing all of this, but that didn't make my heart love him any less—as a friend—because deep down, I knew that's all we could ever be.

I laid down and felt my body melt into the plush pillowtop mattress and closed my eyes. Not only had he bought me new pillows, but he'd also gotten me the softest throw blanket, a warm robe, and some cute house slippers that he insisted I needed because the hardwood floors got cold at night.

I hadn't felt this pampered or cared for in so long that I allowed myself to relish in it for the night before facing reality in the morning.

Knowing that Kennedy was safely asleep in the room next to me, I closed my eyes and drifted off into the most peaceful sleep I'd had in years.

The next morning, I was woken up by the heavenly aroma of coffee and bacon floating through the air. There was a chill in the room, so I grabbed the robe he'd left out for me and slipped on the house slippers.

When I got to the kitchen, I found Kennedy sitting at the island, laughing as Sam flipped a pancake in the air before catching it in the pan.

"Again! Again!" she squealed, pure happiness on her face.

I stood beside her and grinned as I watched Sam repeat his trick for her. I bent down and kissed the top of her head, gently touching my hand against her forehead to check for a fever. Thankfully, she didn't feel warm, and the color on her face made it look like she was feeling a lot better.

"Sam flips pancakes high in the air, Mom!" she exclaimed, her blue eyes wide as they looked up at me.

"I see that," I replied happily. "He's really good at it."

"You don't want to see how many are in the pile for Jake," he said, glancing over his shoulder as he placed the pancake on top of the stack on the plate.

"Who's Jake?"

"The neighbor's dog."

"You feed your neighbor's dog?" I asked with a giggle as I sat down beside Kennedy.

"Yeah, I bribe him with treats every now and then. He's old and crotchety, just like his owner. I've found that sweets tend to keep me on both of their good sides."

"Good to know." I nodded my head, wondering what kind of dog it was and whether I needed to keep Kennedy away from it. She was *obsessed* with dogs, which meant she would now be obsessed with this one.

"What kind of dog is it?" she asked around a mouthful of pancake. *Called it.*

"He's a pug. Ugly little thing that likes to drool all over, but cute once you get to know him."

He winked to let her know he was playing.

"I checked her temperature this morning, and she was fever-free. I hope you don't mind that I started breakfast. We didn't want to wake you, and she promised me that you give her pancakes and bacon for breakfast every day."

I raised an eyebrow and looked down at my daughter as she looked up at me with the cutest grin.

"You're such a sucker, Sam," I said with a laugh. "She loves pancakes and bacon, but we limit it to like once a week." I reached over and gently tickled her sides, loving how she giggled.

"You tricked me?" he asked with his hand over his heart as if he'd been shot. "The betrayal."

"Sorry," Kennedy sang as she happily chewed the piece of bacon hanging from her mouth.

"I don't think you are. You just use me for pancakes and bacon," he whined, pretending to cry. "Then convince me that your mom said it was okay to have hot chocolate for breakfast while watching cartoons!"

My eyes widened even more as I looked down at Kennedy, not believing my ears.

"Kennedy!" I hissed, wondering what had come over her. Being cheeky was fine, but telling lies to get what she wanted wasn't something I tolerated.

"I'm just kidding," Sam rushed out, holding his hand up to stop me. "She didn't ask for any of that. I was just getting back at her for her tricking me with breakfast."

I narrowed my eyes, looking from him to her. They were going to be trouble together, I just knew it.

"I don't know who to believe," I teased. "It seems like there's lots of fibbing happening in here."

"Well, technically, she started it," Sam said, pointing a spatula at Kennedy and causing her to giggle again.

"That doesn't surprise me one bit."

"Mama, can I be done?" she asked, tugging on the arm of my robe to get my attention.

"Is your tummy full?" I had no idea how much she had eaten since she'd started before I came out.

"Yep."

"Alright. You can be done. Please ask Sam where you can clear your plate."

She hopped down from her chair and I handed her the plastic plate he had given her with her food. He showed her where the trashcan was and then helped her load the plate into the dishwasher.

"Can I watch *The Grinch?*" she asked, eyes hopeful as she looked between us.

"We just watched it last night," I said softly, not wanting Sam to go out of his mind with having to watch the same thing over and over.

"Yeah, but I missed some of it because I was sleeping."

"I know, but we don't want to bore Sam with watching it again."

"I don't mind," he said softly, his eyes locking onto mine.

"Okay. But just once. Then, after that, we'll take a shower and get cleaned up."

"Okay, momma." She smiled and then bounced into the living room, clearly feeling better.

I was going to get up to go turn on the TV, but Sam beat me to it.

"Do you want your hot chocolate with green marshmallows?" he asked her as he headed back to the kitchen.

My jaw dropped open, knowing she had been trying to convince him to give her hot chocolate after all.

"Yes, please! And whipped cream!"

I shook my head at him as I tried to keep the smile off my face.

"Oh, you are in so much trouble," I teased.

"What?" He shrugged while sporting the cutest ear-to-ear smile. "I want to be the fun, cool uncle. Gotta get those brownie points in somehow, or I'll never beat Cassidy."

"You're in a competition with Cassidy over who Kennedy likes more?"

"Yeah, but she doesn't know it yet, so don't say anything. Okay?"

"First, you lie to me about my kid conning you into a breakfast filled with sugar, and then you ask me to lie to my best friend?" I gasped and clutched my hand to my chest. "Talk about betrayal."

"Hey, I bought you five new pillows—you should've seen the bribes coming."

"And here I was, foolishly thinking you just did that because you're such a good guy."

"I am. But I also want to win." He winked, and it immediately sent jolts of electricity through my body in a way I hadn't felt in years.

"I can't believe what I'm hearing. If Cassidy knew what you were doing…." I pointed my finger at him and tsked. "And so close to Christmas!"

He leaned forward on the island and held my gaze.

"Would a peppermint mocha be enough to change your mind this morning?"

"Now you're bringing lattes into the mix?" I leaned back and folded my arms over my chest. "Sam. Sam. Sam."

"Alright. Alright. You drive a hard bargain." He picked up the towel that was sitting on the counter and tossed it over his shoulder. "How about a gingerbread latte? Final offer."

My stomach growled loudly before I could answer, which made Sam's eyes light up. He spun around and grabbed a plate before quickly piling it with bacon and pancakes.

"I'll even add in breakfast," he teased with a flirty smirk.

I tipped my head back and sighed heavily as if all of this was too much of a burden.

"Fine. But when Cassidy unfriends me because I succumbed to her brother's crazy competition, I'm going to blame it on the lattes."

"Hey, I only offered one. You can't blame it on all of them."

"If you want me to keep your dirty little secrets, there will be unlimited lattes in my future." I waggled my brows, but when he licked his lips, I knew I was in trouble.

52

<u>Nine</u>

Sam

Avery moans when she enjoys what she's eating, which basically meant that my dick now identified as an all-you-can-eat buffet. I tried desperately to ignore the sounds and not focus on how she looked with her eyes closed and lips slightly parted as she devoured dinner, but it was hard. Literally hard.

After dinner, I cleaned up while Avery and Kennedy decided on which movie to watch. We had decided that we were going to watch one Christmas movie every night from now until Christmas, which left us with a lot of movies to choose from. I initially voted for *Die Hard* but then retracted when I remembered that Kennedy didn't need to go around telling anyone, "Yippee-ki-yay mother fucker" and that it was a bit violent. We'd settled on *Miracle On 34th Street,* and I was surprised to hear that Avery had never seen it.

We settled in on the couch with Kennedy cuddled under a mountain of blankets between us as we watched the movie. I'd made popcorn and didn't tell Avery that I had purchased twelve of those movie theater-sized candy boxes until they were scattered around the ottoman with the other snacks. She pretended to be mad, but her smile gave her away as she reached for the Hot Tamales and popped a handful into her mouth.

She didn't moan with them the way she did with the fried chicken and mashed potatoes, but I was impressed that she also didn't seem bothered by how spicy they were. Maybe I was a wimp because I could only handle a few at a time without my eyes tearing up and my mouth catching on fire. I didn't want to allow myself to think about all the things Avery's mouth could handle because that was a deep, slippery slope I had no place being on.

Once the movie was over, Avery got Kennedy to bed while I sat in the living room, unsure whether she was going to call it a night herself. It was barely after eight, but I knew Avery had been more tired than usual lately, so I didn't want her to feel obligated to stay up with me.

I was washing out the containers we'd used for snacks when I heard Avery come into the kitchen.

"Do you need help?" she asked, trying to stifle a yawn.

"I'm done, but thank you."

She nodded and looked around the kitchen, which was now spotless.

"I don't think I've ever met a man who kept his house as clean as you do."

"I'm going to take that as a compliment," I teased as I hung the towel on the hook and leaned against the counter to look at her.

"You should. It's a huge compliment. So many men don't care about all of the little things, but you do, and it shows. Someday, you're going to make one woman very happy."

My heart jumped at the thought that possibly she meant deep down that woman would be her.

"Are you staying up for a bit?" I asked, trying to get a feel for what she wanted to do.

"Yeah. I'm tired but not ready for bed just yet."

"Want to watch a movie?"

"That depends…" Her smile made her brown eyes light up.

"Are you about to con me into a late-night latte or pancakes and bacon like your daughter?" I asked playfully, pointing a finger at her.

"Oh, heck no. I don't do caffeine this late unless I want to be up all night. The only exception I make is if it's an Irish coffee, and even then, I usually go for decaf coffee."

"I can make that happen." I looked past her to the shelf that held my assorted collection of whiskey.

"I'm not trying to con you into making me a drink, Sam," she said with a laugh as she walked past and swatted my arm. "I am, however, going to sneak into the snacks I bought the other day, BUT you cannot tell Kennedy that I ate them."

My jaw dropped and hung open as she reached into the pantry and pulled out a family-sized bag of Cheetos.

"Okay—I know we've had a lot of deceit happening in here the past twenty-four hours, but you have got to be kidding me. You're seriously asking me to keep a secret from Kennedy?"

She opened the bag, stood right in front of me, and pulled a Cheeto out. She looked me dead in the eye as she slowly parted her lips and placed it inside her mouth. I tried desperately not to be fixated on her mouth or on how she was so close I could smell the sweet fragrance of her shampoo.

The Cheeto crunched loudly as she chewed, continuing the stare down.

I shook my head, forcing myself to break free from the spell she had me under as I shoved a hand through my hair.

"Fine. If I'm keeping your secret, you're going to have to keep mine and not be mad about it."

She stepped back slowly, a smirk crossing her lips as she frowned, wondering what I was up to.

"I won't tell Kennedy that you had Cheetos after dinner if you promise you won't be upset when I show you what I got her."

"Like for Christmas?" she asked, her head tilted in confusion. "You didn't have to get her anything for Christmas, Sam. I don't know if we'll even be here—"

"Stop," I said, holding my hand up. "You will be here for Christmas, and I will buy *both* of you gifts. Fighting me on it won't do anything but increase your frustration when you find you won't get your way with me."

"Sam—"

"Nope. Na uh. I don't want to hear it. Now, before I show you what I got her, do you promise not to be mad?"

"I can't promise anything. For all I know, you went crazy and bought her a pony."

I shook my head and scrunched my nose.

"No, no ponies. They're too messy, and she's too little to really enjoy them. Maybe next year."

"Sam…" Her voice came through as a warning.

I grimaced and opened the door to the garage, knowing she was going to either love what I did or hate it.

"Now remember, you can't be mad."

She raised her eyebrows and set the bag of Cheetos down on the counter.

I reached inside and grabbed the two large bags from Waldon's that I had gotten yesterday.

I didn't think it was even possible, but her eyebrows rose even higher.

"What in the world is in there?" she asked, hands planted firmly on her hips.

I took a deep breath and steadied my hands as I pulled the box out of the bag and set it down in between us.

She went from shocked to confused in a matter of seconds.

"I know you weren't planning to stay for Christmas, but I would really love it if you would reconsider," I said softly, lifting the box with the light pink mini Christmas tree. "I thought it would be fun for Kennedy to have her own tree in her room that she could decorate. I know this isn't the home she's used to, but I don't see why we can't try to make it feel like home for her while she's here."

Avery covered her mouth with her hands as tears filled her eyes.

"Sam, you didn't have—"

"I know. I wanted to, Avery."

I gave her a few minutes while she wiped at her eyes, overwhelmed with emotion.

"I thought maybe tomorrow the three of us could decorate the house. My tree is up, but I haven't had time to put lights or ornaments on and could really use the help."

Her lower lip quivered as she nodded yes.

It was a small victory, but at least one small step headed in the right direction.

Ten
Avery

I woke up to my head pounding and my body aching. I pulled the blanket tighter around me, shivering against the cold. I had no idea what time it was, but my body desperately wanted more sleep.

I heard Kennedy's soft voice and knew that wasn't an option. She was up, which meant I needed to get up. I climbed out of bed and pulled on an extra hoodie, hoping that would help warm me up. When I stopped in the bathroom to relieve myself, I noticed the pale color of my skin and knew that I had caught whatever it was that Kennedy had.

It sucked being sick, but moms didn't get sick days, so I brushed my teeth, splashed some cold water on my face, and told myself that I would make the best of today.

By the time I got to the kitchen, I found Sam at the stove making scrambled eggs. The smell immediately made me queasy as I leaned down to kiss Kennedy on the head.

"Good morning," I said, taking a seat beside her as a shiver ran through me.

"Morni—" Sam started but then stopped when he saw me. "Woah. Are you okay?"

"Is that your polite way of saying I look like shit this morning?" I teased, trying to force my eyes open.

"Not at all." He turned the burner off and removed the pan from the heat as he walked over and stood in front of me. His eyes quickly scanned my face as he lifted his hand and rested it against my forehead.

"Avery, you're burning up."

"I know. I think I caught what Kennedy had. Don't stand too close. I don't want to give it to you, too," I warned, trying to pull away from his touch but slightly losing my balance on the chair. His hands reached out and steadied me.

"I could care less about getting sick," he said softly. "I care about you and getting you well. You should go back to bed and rest."

"Thank you, but I can't do that."

"Why not?"

I glanced down at Kennedy and raised my eyebrows so he would get the point.

"I can take care of Kennedy," he offered. "We'll have a fun day together."

"I appreciate the offer," I replied before stopping to cough into my arm. "But really, I'm fine."

"You're not fine, Avery. Not by a long shot. You need rest, fluids, and some medicine to break that fever."

"All stuff I can do while I'm awake and taking care of her," I objected.

"I have to go potty," Kennedy said, interrupting us.

I smiled as Sam helped her down from the chair before she rushed off down the hallway, more comfortable here than she had been at our old house.

"Look, I know you're just trying to help, but you don't have to," I said while Kennedy was out of ear shot. "I'm used to doing this while I'm sick. It's just part of being a mom."

"While I appreciate and respect that, I'm telling you that you don't *have* to. I'm here and happy to help. Trust me, she will be fine with me taking care of her. If it makes you feel better, I'll call Cassidy and ask her for help. But I'm not going to stand here and fight with you on this. You need rest, and one way or another, I'm going to make sure you get it."

"Sam," I objected with a heavy breath.

He pinned me with a look as he pulled his phone out of his pocket. His fingers moved quickly across the screen before he pressed it to his ear and waited, eyes still glued firmly to mine.

"Hey, Cass. Avery is sick and I'm taking care of Kennedy today. Do you want to come have hot chocolate and lots of junk food while we decorate my house?"

I stared at him in disbelief, attempting to shake my head at him until a sneeze overcame me.

"Cool. I'll see you in half an hour. Be sure to stop by Sugarplum Sweets and get some of those truffles and sugar cookies."

I pointed a finger at him in warning, letting him know he was going to be in trouble for all of the sweets when he decided to up the ante.

"Be sure to get the ones we can decorate ourselves. I'm sure Kennedy will love eating the frosting and decorations as she tries to put them on the cookies."

He grinned as he ended the call and put it back into his pocket.

"Oh, you're so going to pay for all of this," I warned, trying to stand up but losing my balance again.

"You can make me pay all you want later. But for now, you're going to take some medicine and go back to bed."

His hand was warm on my lower back as he guided me back to bed.

Eleven
Sam

"It's really nice of you to do all of this," Cassidy said, smiling as we watched Kennedy smear more red frosting on her sugar cookie. "But Avery is totally going to kill you when she sees this mess."

"Then I guess it's a good thing she's still sleeping and that I'll have it cleaned up before she gets up."

"Do you want me to stay over tonight and help with Kennedy so Avery can rest?"

I shoved a hand through my hair and looked down at the little girl who was now covered in red, green, and yellow frosting. I wanted Avery to trust that I could handle taking care of her daughter, but at the same time, I hadn't been around a child since Cassidy was little. It was a lot to take in, and I didn't want to mess things up.

"Would you mind?"

"Not at all. I'm off tomorrow anyway, so it works out. Is Avery scheduled to work tomorrow?"

"Yeah, but I called Piper this morning and let her know that she's sick. She's checking with some of the part-time employees to see if anyone can fill in for her."

"I'm sure she'll be upset about missing work, but it's for

the better. She's in no condition to try to do anything right now."

"Why will she be upset?" I asked, lowering my voice so Kennedy didn't hear as I stepped back into the living room, hoping my sister would follow.

"She's trying to get enough money to start her Christmas shopping, so she was really looking forward to her first paycheck."

"And now it's going to be short," I commented, putting the pieces together.

"It's okay. I'm supposed to get a Christmas bonus next week, so I can always give that to her. It won't be much, but something is better than nothing."

"Do you think she would be mad if we put her name on the gifting tree at the mall?"

Cassidy shrugged and looked over at Kennedy.

"Even if she is, she can't stay mad forever. Plus, the more gifts we can get for them, the better. It breaks my heart not being able to buy for them the way I want to."

"I know. Me too."

****

Cassidy helped clean up the mess and then got Kennedy into a bath before Avery woke up and saw her covered in frosting. I hadn't been able to stop thinking about what Cassidy had said about Avery needing money to start shopping for Kennedy. I didn't usually give Christmas bonuses at Sugarplum Lattes because we always had an elaborate holiday party instead. Still, I kept getting a nagging feeling about changing things this year.

While Cassidy sat curled up on the couch with Kennedy, watching a movie, I sat at the kitchen table, looking over the reports from the past three years on what I'd spent on the holiday parties. It was roughly the same every year, which was nice because at least I had an amount to go off of. Between renting a ballroom at the Sugarplum Suites for the party, having a plated dinner, and offering everyone two drink vouchers, I was spending a lot. If I took that money and divided it among all of the employees, I could give everyone a very healthy cash bonus this year instead.

I grabbed a piece of paper and wrote down everyone's names, making sure that Piper got a slightly larger bonus for the extra work she'd been doing. Not only did she run a tight ship when I wasn't there and kept things in line, but she was also going in on her days off to cover shifts when we needed it.

By the time I had everything written down, I smiled at the paper and felt a warmth spread through me. By eliminating the holiday party this year, I would be able to give everyone a five-hundred-dollar cash bonus this week.

Twelve

Avery

"I need to go to work," I objected, trying to get past Sam, who blocked me in the kitchen.

"Not today, Avery."

"You don't get it," I mumbled, still feeling way too tired to try to function. But that didn't matter right now. If I was going to make Christmas magical for Kennedy, I needed every penny I could get.

"I do. And I'm sorry you're feeling frustrated, but you're no good to me at work like this. You need to sleep and get better."

"I'm fine. Really. I'm going to work if you'd move out of the way so I can get my shoes." I sniffled, then burst into a coughing fit.

"You need to rest, momma," Kennedy said, tugging on my hand to get my attention.

"See, even Kennedy knows you need to rest," Cassidy said, walking past me and opening the refrigerator.

"How did you get here?" I asked, feeling like I was in a fever dream again. I had tossed and turned so much that I couldn't tell if it was day or night when I finally woke up.

"I've been here since yesterday. I brought treats from Sugarplum Sweets. I helped Sam and Kennedy decorate those sugar cookies." She nodded to the plate sitting on the island. "And I stayed the night after helping with dinner and giving Kennedy a bath. I've been here the whole time."

I shook my head, only making myself dizzier.

"Well, then, you can drive me to work."

"Nope. No can do. You, my friend, are staying home today."

"You guys are impossible," I groaned, throwing my head back in frustration.

"No, you are being impossible," Cassidy corrected, pinning me with a look. "You're sick, and believe it or not, no one wants a shot of flu with their espresso. So stay home and get better. I'm sure Sam will have opportunities for you to make up your hours once you're feeling better."

"She's right," Sam said, giving me a gentle smile. "This time of year gets super busy, and we always have days when we need extra help. It will be easy to make up the hours you're missing today."

I looked down at my daughter, who was pleading with her eyes and begging me to stay.

"Alright. Fine." I sighed and pulled her in for a hug as her hands wrapped around my hips.

"Do you want me to make you breakfast, momma?"

"No, honey. Thank you. I'll make *you* breakfast, though. What would you like?"

"Sam already made me pancakes and bacon," she said, dancing happily around me.

I looked up and found him grinning.

"I said it was a once-a-week thing," I playfully scolded. "Not an everyday thing."

"I'm sorry, Avery. I tried. I really did. But then she looked at me with those big, blue eyes, and I couldn't say no."

"You're gonna have to try harder."

"Or I could just stay the cool, fun uncle," he teased, winking at me.

"Are you and Cassidy still fighting to be Kennedy's favorite?"

The words had slipped out before I could process them.

Sam's eyes widened as Cassidy's narrowed at me.

"What?" she demanded, planting her hands on her hips and glaring at him. "You're purposely doing stuff to get Kennedy to like you more?"

"No," he lied, transforming from the innocent brother sad face to the irresistibly cute pretend angry face he was giving me.

"You liar! I knew it! That's why you took credit for the sugar cookies yesterday."

"Hey, I took credit for them because they were my idea. You can ask Avery. She was standing right here when I asked you to get them."

"Yeah, but *I* was the one who bought them. I should get credit for that."

"You only bought them because *I* told you to."

"Whatever." Cassidy huffed out a breath and folded her arms over her chest as she turned away from her brother.

"You can't act like you haven't been trying to bribe Kennedy as well," Sam said, pointing a finger at his sister. "You're the one who brought the bath crayons and let her draw all over the walls of the tub last night. You're also the one who bought the Christmas-themed fruit snacks and made Christmas-shaped Rice Krispie treats."

"Hey—she liked them," Cassidy objected, whirling around to glare at her brother.

"Of course she did. But what you mean to say is that she liked *you*."

"You're damn right she does. I'm her favorite aunt."

"You're her only aunt," I corrected, only to back away as Cassidy turned her glare to me.

"Whose side are you on?" she demanded, arching an eyebrow.

"Ummm, no one?"

"Oh, is that so?" Sam said, giving me a look of his own. "Should we start telling Kennedy *your* secrets?"

My mouth opened in disbelief before I quickly snapped it shut.

"You have secrets, Mommy?" Kennedy asked, looking up at me in confusion.

"No, baby. Mommy doesn't have any secrets. Sam is just being silly."

"Are you sure about that?" he teased, heading to the pantry.

My eyes widened as I shook my head no. He opened the door and pulled out the bag of Cheetos I had been eating the other night.

"Allow me to present exhibit A to you," he said, setting the Cheetos down on the island.

"Did you eat Cheetos without me?" Kennedy asked, looking at me with a frown on her face.

Before I could answer, Sam beat me to it.

"She did. *After* you went to bed."

"Sam!" I exclaimed at the same time as Cassidy.

He jumped back, startled by our outbursts, as Kennedy started laughing.

"Oooh, Sam is in trouble," she giggled.

"Me? What about your mom? She ate Cheetos without you while you were sleeping."

"Yeah, but she's an adult. She can do whatever she wants," Kennedy said with a small shrug. "Plus, she ate the ones she likes. If she ate the puffy ones I like, then I might be mad."

"So, what you're saying is that the puffy Cheetos are the key to winning this thing?" Sam said, contemplating a little too hard.

"Oh, you two knock it off," I said, shaking my head. "She loves both of you equally. Now stop fighting over who her favorite is because we all know that it's me."

I bent down and picked her up, knowing she was far too heavy for me to hold right now. I sat her on my hip and brushed my nose against hers, loving the way her arms wrapped around my neck to give me the biggest hug ever.

Thirteen

Sam

"I thought you guys were going to decorate yesterday?" Avery asked, sitting on the couch sipping the hot tea I'd made for her.

"Kennedy and I both agreed that we wanted to wait for you. I haven't shown her the *other thing* yet," I replied, making sure Kennedy didn't hear.

I had wanted to give Kennedy her tree but decided to wait until Avery was feeling better so she could be a part of it. Plus, today was officially twelve days until Christmas, which made it even better to wait until today to give it to her since I'd gotten her a twelve days of Christmas ornament set. Each ornament was hidden in an advent-style calendar, and she opened one a day until Christmas. I hadn't told Avery about the ornaments yet, but I couldn't imagine she would be upset about it.

She spent the morning in bed resting, as we had asked, then came out about an hour ago, looking much better with color flushing her cheeks again. I'd gotten her to eat a light breakfast and was thankful she seemed to be past the worst of it.

"She's going to love it," Avery said with a smile as she watched Kennedy and Cassidy finish the puzzle they were working on that Cassidy had brought over yesterday.

"I hope so." I hated that I felt so unsure about it because deep down, I wanted nothing more than to see the happiness on Kennedy's face when she saw it.

"Finished!" Kennedy said, standing up and staring down at the puzzle on the coffee table with pride.

"Great job, sweetheart!" Avery exclaimed, setting her tea on the end table beside her as she leaned forward to see the puzzle. "It looks amazing!"

"Thank you, momma. It was fun but a little too easy." She scrunched her nose playfully as Cassidy pretended to be offended.

"Fine, next time, I'm getting one of those 3D ones that take months to finish," Cassidy said, getting up off the floor.

Kennedy giggled and curled up on the couch next to Avery.

"You taking off?" I asked my sister as I saw her grab her purse from the coat rack.

"Yeah. I need to do laundry and get ready for work this week. It's a lot harder when things aren't where I expect them to be at Mom's house. I swear, she and Dad get bored and move stuff around just for fun. It took me twenty minutes to find the dryer sheets the other day because Mom moved them to this decorative box, as if dryer sheets were some secret thing we needed to keep hidden."

"Well, we're going to start decorating the house if you want to stay and help us," I offered.

"Thanks, but I had to help Mom and Dad decorate theirs, so I think I'm maxed out this year. Did you know that there is a *wrong* way to hang Christmas lights?" Cassidy sighed heavily as she shrugged on her coat and pulled a beanie over her head.

"I absolutely do believe it. I'm a firm believer in hanging lights the right way."

"You're weird, just like Dad."

"That's not a nice word," Kennedy said, scowling at Cassidy.

"I'm sorry. You're right. It's not a nice word."

"Are you going to apologize?" Kennedy pushed, raising her eyebrows in a way that made her look just like Avery.

Cassidy looked from Kennedy to me and then shook her head.

"Nope. Sorry, kiddo, but Sam deserves it." She winked to let Kennedy know she was just playing as she elbowed me in the ribs on her way over to hug her. "I'll see you later this week. Be good for your momma."

"I will."

"Call if you need anything," Cassidy said as I walked her to the door. "I already let Mom know you guys wouldn't be there for dinner tonight. I'm sure she'll have me bring food over later."

"Please tell her not to worry about it. I'm not sure what Avery will be in the mood for, and I want her to take it easy on her stomach. But thank Mom for the offer, please."

"Will do. See you later. Love you."

I gave my sister a giant bear hug and then watched to make

sure she got to her car safely. The sky was bright white, which meant the winter storm was coming quickly.

I closed the door and locked it before turning up the thermostat. I wanted to make sure the girls stayed nice and warm, especially if the weatherman was right and we were about to get walloped with a few feet of snow. It wasn't anything out of the ordinary for Sugarplum Falls, but this was more snow than we usually got at one time.

"Alright, ladies," I said as I walked back into the living room, rubbing my hands together. "Let's start decorating!"

Fourteen

Avery

I had never heard Kennedy giggle as much as she did with Sam while they attempted to put tinsel on the tree. I told them it was a bad idea, but they didn't listen.

Tinsel covered the carpet and most of Kennedy's hair, with very little of it actually making its way on the tree. But Kennedy was having fun and smiling, which was the only thing that mattered right now.

I was finally feeling better and had more strength and energy than before, which was refreshing. I'd taken Sam's advice and added a dash of whiskey to my tea—something I wouldn't typically have done because of Kennedy. But having Sam there and seeing how good he was with her allowed me to lower my guard a little bit and accept his help with her.

Once the tree was trimmed and every inch of the house was decorated, we sat down on the couch to catch our breath. Kennedy curled into my side, and I was reminded of how blessed I was to have her as my daughter.

"Thank you, ladies, for your help. The house looks Christmas-tastic!" Sam said with a huge grin as he struggled to hide something behind the couch. "I have one last thing that I need Kennedy's help with."

"Me?" she asked, looking from him to me.

I smiled and nodded for her to go see what he had for her. She climbed off the couch and rushed over. Her eyes lit up like fireworks as he picked up the mini Christmas tree and set it in front of her.

"A pink Christmas tree?!" she exclaimed. "And it's my size!"

"That's because it's your special Christmas tree. I thought we could put it in your room and you could take care of decorating it. There's also this box of ornaments that you open one per day until Christmas."

"My own tree in my own room?! This is so exciting! I can't believe we get to live here forever!" Kennedy squealed as she hugged the tree tightly and swung it gently.

My heart sank in my chest as I heard her words, not wanting to break her heart by correcting her. Our stay with Sam was temporary, and we all knew that. Or at least I thought we did.

Sam helped her take the tree to her room while I sat on the couch, trying to get myself together. It wasn't his fault that she made that assumption. It was mine for not properly communicating to her that we didn't have a place to call home yet. I knew that I needed to figure something out, and soon, but it wasn't that easy. I wanted to make sure that we had the best start possible, and that meant I had to take the time to figure out what that was. She was too little to know or understand everything that had happened, and I wanted to keep it that way.

A few minutes later, Sam came back with a sheepish smile on his face.

"I'm so sorry, Avery. I didn't mean for that to happen. When I thought about getting her the tree for her room, it never even crossed my mind that she might think this was a permanent home. Not that I mind you guys staying with me, because I don't. You can stay for as long as you want to. I have no timeframe in mind on when you two have to—"

"Sam?" I said, forcing him to stop on the downward spiral he was on.

"Yeah?"

"It's okay. I promise. It's not your fault she came to that conclusion. It's my error in not setting expectations right away that our stay here was only temporary. I've been so caught up with everything else that I haven't even taken the time to think about how she must be perceiving all of this. So much has changed for her in such a short time that I forget to stop and help her process all of it."

"You've had a lot going on, Avery. I don't think anyone faults you for not knowing how long you'll be here. But you're right. She has had a lot of change in a short period. Maybe this is when things slow down some, and you both take a moment to catch your breath. Nobody expects you to have the next step figured out already."

"I do," I said with a laugh. "The day I packed up the car and left with Kennedy, I told myself that I would keep pushing forward until we had a sign that we were where we were meant to be. I knew it would be hard to walk away from the life that we knew, but we had to. It was the only choice we had. And now here I am, falling apart and having no idea where to go or what to do." I sucked in a deep breath to keep from crying.

Sam came and sat beside me on the couch.

"You're not falling apart, Avery. You're taking care of your daughter and leaning on family to help you guys through this trying time right now. Like I said before, there is no time limit on how long you guys stay here. Trust me."

"Thank you, Sam. You don't have to do all of this, though."

"I know. I want to."

I wiped my eyes and smiled as I took the tissue he offered me.

"This would be so much easier if you were my cheating husband who didn't love me anymore," I teased, though I felt the sting of my words as I said them.

Sam's face fell, and a flurry of emotions crossed over it before he pushed them away.

"That would never happen, Avery," he said, his voice tight.

"I know," I said, waving dismissively. "I wasn't trying to suggest that you would ever see yourself married to someone like me."

"No. I could easily see myself married to someone like you. What I meant is that I would never be that person, Avery. I would never cheat on someone as wonderful as you, and there's no way in hell that I could ever *not* love you."

The air in the room shifted around us as he stood up and left me sitting speechless on the couch.

Fifteen
Sam

"First, I would like to thank everyone for coming in this evening for this very last-minute meeting." I smiled through the groaning I heard in the back. "I know you all have better things to do, but I have an important announcement and wanted everyone to be here for it."

I felt Piper's eyes on me and knew she was nervous about whatever was about to happen since I hadn't talked to her about it. But that was the fun part about doing surprises like this.

"I know that it's late notice, but I've decided to cancel this year's holiday party."

There was a collective gasp as people started whispering amongst themselves.

"I don't know whether a lot of you were looking forward to it or not, given that Piper has only gotten a few RSVPs for it, and it's literally in a week. But either way, it has been canceled."

Piper looked down nervously, and I hated that I had put the spotlight on her, but it was true. Very few people had bothered to tell her whether they were coming, and those who did hadn't given her an answer on whether they were bringing a plus one. Trying to get anyone to commit to anything was like pulling teeth. I had great employees for the most part, but I also knew that a lot of them had second jobs or were in school, so they constantly had a lot on their plates, which made committing to something like a holiday party that much harder.

"Since the holiday party is canceled, I've decided to take the money that we would have spent on the party and turned it into holiday bonuses for everyone instead."

I grinned as the energy in the room immediately shifted.

"Piper, would you help me pass these out?" I asked, handing her half the stack of envelopes.

We worked quickly to get them distributed, and my heart was filled with happiness as I heard the excitement when they started opening them and saw how much their checks were.

"That's it for the meeting," I said loudly, trying to pull their attention back to me so I could end the meeting and officially close up for the day. "Thank you all for your hard work. I greatly appreciate it."

I was met with hugs as everyone made their way back to the front of the shop to leave. Once they were gone, Piper waited for me in my office.

"That was a very kind thing you did with the bonuses," she said softly, still holding her envelope in her hand. "I appreciate the gesture, but I cannot accept this."

She attempted to hand it back to me, but I leaned back in my chair and folded my hands over my stomach.

"Yes, you can. And you will. You earned that bonus, Piper."

"It's double what you gave everyone else, Sam."

"Were you peaking over their shoulders?" I teased, eyeing her suspiciously.

"I mean, some of them are short. I couldn't help that I saw the amount."

I raised my eyebrows as I pretended to judge her.

"But still, I can't accept this, Sam. Not when you've given everyone a bonus but won't take one for yourself."

"You don't know that."

"Yes, I do. I've worked with you for five years, and I have never seen you do something nice for yourself. You're always worried about taking care of everyone else, but who takes care of you?"

That was a loaded question if I ever heard one.

"Hey, sorry to interrupt," Avery said, knocking on the doorframe. "I know you asked everyone to go home, but is it okay if I stay to close up? I could use the extra hours to make up for my sick day."

She's who takes care of me.

I shook my head to clear the errant thought and tried to focus.

"Yes. That's fine. I'll be out there in a few to help."

She smiled and walked out.

"I'm serious, Sam. Please take the check back. I can't accept it, knowing that you are the only one going without a bonus this year. Out of everyone, you deserve it the most."

"I'm the owner, Piper. My bonus is the joy I get out of seeing my business thrive."

She rolled her eyes and tossed her envelope on my desk.

"You're so full of shit that it's starting to stink in here. I'm going home and will be in early to open in the morning. Fix that, and then I'll consider accepting it. Give me the same as everyone else, or even less. Doesn't matter to me. But I'm not taking that large of a bonus unless you do, too." She nodded to her bonus and then turned to leave.

I pulled the checkbook out of my desk drawer and flipped it open.

"There. Happy?" I asked, lifting it to show her my name written on the payee line with the same amount as what I gave her.

"Sign it and tear it off."

I rolled my eyes and then finished writing the check before tearing it off and handing it to her.

"Thank you. I'll drop these off at the bank in the morning along with the deposit."

"Sounds good," I said with a heavy sigh, just to let her know how much I didn't like it.

She grinned and waved as she headed out.

When I got up front, Avery was wiping down the counters, and the supplies were fully restocked for the morning.

"Wow. You work fast," I said, impressed with how much she got done in such a short time.

"I'm a mom. You learn to get things done quickly when you're trying to balance keeping a clean house and taking care of a baby. It kinda just sticks with you."

"Well, I appreciate your help tonight."

"And I appreciate the bonus." She stopped and looked at me, her head tilted as if she was trying to figure something out.

"Why do I get the feeling that this new bonus thing is because of me?"

I chewed my lower lip as I tried to figure out what the best approach to this would be.

"It's not," I lied.

"Really?"

I nodded, not trusting my words to come out clearly right now.

"People didn't seem interested in the holiday party this year, so I figured I might as well do something better with the money. Times can get pretty tough this time of year, and it feels good to help out however I can."

"Yeah, but you've never done a bonus until I started working for you."

"True. But maybe you working for me has helped me see things differently. You can't fault me for trying to be the good guy who wants to help his employees, Avery."

"I'm not," she rushed out quickly with a shake of her head. "But I also can't help but feel guilty, like I'm the reason you had to shell out all of that cash in Christmas bonuses."

"I was going to spend that money on the employees one way or another. This just felt like the better way to do it."

"Well, for what it's worth, thank you."

"You're welcome."

We stood there, inches apart for what felt like forever, as she looked down to avoid looking me in the eye.

"So," I said, trying to break the awkward silence. "Cassidy said she would watch Kenndy overnight tonight. I thought maybe if you wanted to, we could go grab dinner and then do some Christmas shopping."

"Oh. Umm. I don't know. I mean, it sounds fun, but I can't really do that right now."

Her cheeks flushed crimson, and I hated myself for being so clueless. She hadn't gotten her first paycheck from me yet because she started at the beginning of a new pay cycle, which meant she couldn't afford to go out and do fun stuff right now.

I turned on my heel and headed for my office, ready to solve the problem. I could hear her still cleaning up in the front as I pulled the petty cash box out of the safe and unlocked it. Thankfully, we kept enough in there that I was able to cash her bonus check out without leaving it empty.

I grabbed the cash and headed up front, rounding the corner at the same time she did.

Her soft body crashed against mine as my hand reached out to steady her.

"Sorry, I didn't see you there," she mumbled, her breasts pressed firmly against my chest.

"You're fine. I shouldn't have been in such a rush. Are you okay?"

"Yeah," she breathed out, her voice a little shaky as she made no effort to move away from me.

My hand rubbed down her back as my fingers feathered lightly above her ass. Her back arched as if inviting me to touch it while her head lifted slightly to see me.

Without even thinking about it, I dropped the cash in my hand and pulled her against me as my mouth crashed down over hers. She moaned softly, her fingers tangling in my hair as she deepened the kiss.

My tongue swiped against her lip, begging for access as my hands reached down and grabbed her ass. Her chest rose and fell heavily against mine as she jumped up and wrapped her legs around my waist.

Kissing Avery was far better than anything I could have ever imagined. I walked us over to the counter and set her down while our tongues continued to explore. Her fingers tugged at the bottom of my shirt, desperately trying to pull it off when I finally stepped back and broke the kiss.

Her eyes were wide as they studied me, unsure of what just happened.

I scrubbed my hand down my jaw and took a deep breath.

"I'm sorry," she apologized quickly. "I was out of line and shouldn't have—"

"Avery," I interrupted. "Stop."

She closed her mouth and rubbed her swollen lips together.

"You're not the one who needs to be apologizing," I said, taking a step back from her. "I shouldn't have done that. I'm sorry. I crossed a line, and I shouldn't have."

"We both crossed the line," she replied sternly, hopping off of the counter and standing in front of me. "It wasn't just you. I wanted that as much as you did."

"You did?"

She nodded.

"I don't know what I'm doing in life right now, Sam, and I'm sure there will be plenty that I regret as I try to figure things out. But kissing you—that's one thing I will never regret."

Sixteen

Avery

I kissed Sam.

Not only did I kiss my best friend's older brother—who I was currently living with, but I enjoyed it more than I could have ever anticipated.

Growing up, I'd always had a crush on Sam but never thought anything could happen between us because he always felt off limits being Cassidy's brother. But now that we were older and spending so much time together, I was struggling to keep that boundary drawn.

We stood there staring at each other for a moment as a million thoughts raced through both of our minds after I admitted I would never regret kissing him. But it was true. There were plenty of things in life I might take back if I could, but feeling his warm lips pressed against mine as his body wrapped around me wasn't one of them.

"I don't regret it either," he finally admitted as a dimpled grin appeared.

"Well, then, I guess that clears that up."

"We still have one problem we need to deal with, though."

My body tensed as I waited for whatever bad news he was about to deliver.

"Okay. What's that."

"I want to take you out tonight. At first, it was just as friends to get some holiday shopping done. But now, if you'd let me, I'd like to make it a date."

My eyes widened with surprise. Sam was asking me out on a date?

"Sam, you don't have to do that," I said softly.

"Do what? Like you? Be so wildly attracted to you that I can't stop obsessing over how beautiful you are. Or is it that I really want to spend time with you, and I would be honored if you would give me the privilege of taking you out?"

"I don't know." I laughed nervously, tugging at the hem of my shirt as I looked away. "All of this just happened out of nowhere. And to be honest, I haven't dated anyone in almost a decade. I don't even know what dating is like anymore. Plus, I have Kennedy to think about, and I know you don't like to hear it, but I don't know how long we're staying in Sugarplum Falls."

"I know." He stepped forward and grabbed my hands, holding them in his. "I'm not asking for anything more than tonight, Avery. I know you have a lot on your plate right now and I would never try to make things more complicated. I adore Kennedy and would never want to make things hard for you with her, either. We can take this one baby step at a time. I'm not asking for forever; I'm just asking for tonight. One night where I can take you out and we can explore whatever this thing is between us."

I pulled my lower lip between my teeth and inhaled sharply.

"Don't do that," he warned, his eyes suddenly darkening.

"Do what?" I asked, my voice so soft it was barely audible.

He stepped even closer, releasing my hands as he cupped my face and leaned in.

"Chew on your lip."

"Oh." I meant to release it, but the way he was looking at me so intently only made me bite down on it harder.

He released a frustrated breath before leaning in and devouring my mouth in the most passionate kiss I'd ever had. One hand stayed firmly behind my head while the other wrapped around my body, pulling me flush against him. Even through his jeans, I could feel the defined bulge of his erection.

I whimpered as my body started to turn to mush and a fire spread between my thighs. He hadn't even touched me other than kissing, and I was seconds away from coming undone.

I tried to pull away so I didn't embarrass myself, but then he deepened the kiss, and I was done. I wrapped my arms around his neck and pulled him closer, desperate for whatever he would give me.

He broke the kiss and nudged my head to the side as he mercilessly kissed down my neck and over my collarbone. I was putty in his hands, begging him for the relief I needed.

"Are you sure you want to do this, Avery?" he asked as I clawed at his shirt again.

We were literally in the middle of the coffee shop, acting like two horny teenagers, but I didn't care. I hadn't felt this alive in so long that it gave me a high I didn't want to come down from.

"Yes, Sam. I want it more than anything."

"I don't want you to feel rushed. We can take things slow."

"I don't want slow. I want fast and hard. Possibly bent over this counter or on top of it. I don't care. I just want that *promise of a good time* that keeps poking me through your jeans."

He chuckled and playfully nipped my earlobe.

"A quickie in a coffee shop is not how I ever imagined us doing this," he said with a laugh.

"You've thought about us having sex before?"

I pulled back slightly so I could see his face as he answered.

"Maybe a time or two." He shrugged but didn't give me any of the juicy details I wanted.

"Oh really? And what exactly did you picture when you thought about us having sex?"

"That's for me to know and you to find out."

"Sam!" I exclaimed with a smile stretched so tight across my face that it hurt. "That's not fair. Tell me! Please… I won't tell anyone."

"Neither will I."

I shook my head, frustrated that he was refusing to tell me about it. But then he leaned forward and began kissing my neck again, making me forget all about the other stuff.

His lips were soft and tender as they grazed over my skin, covering it in goosebumps. I reached down and grabbed for the bottom of his shirt again, this time pleased when he allowed me to remove it.

I knew that Sam was gorgeous, but shirtless Sam was my new favorite. My fingers scraped gently down his chest, loving the way his hard pecs felt beneath them before lowering over his defined stomach to the top of his jeans.

"If I'm losing clothes, so are you," he teased, arching an eyebrow.

I lifted the bottom of my shirt and pulled it over my head, revealing a black lace bra as I tossed the shirt to the floor. His eyes leisurely roamed over my body as he licked his lips, making my knees wobbly. I was thankful that there weren't many windows in the store and that the few there were had been frosted and elaborately decorated for the holiday, making them impossible to see through from outside.

"Pants, too," he instructed, stepping closer and invading my space again as the spicy scent of his cologne filled the air between us.

I looked up and locked eyes with him as I unbuttoned my jeans, sliding them slowly down my legs until they were in a puddle at my feet. I stepped out of them, suddenly self-conscious that I was standing in front of him wearing nothing but my bra and panties. Not only that, but the lights were bright enough for him to see the stretchmarks on my stomach from carrying Kennedy.

"You're so beautiful," he said softly, reaching for me and pulling me against him again.

"I'm officially wearing less clothes than you, so I think it's your turn to take something off."

"I will in a minute. But first," he paused as he lifted and set me on the counter, "I want to make you come on my tongue."

I couldn't see my face, so I had no idea what it looked like. But if I had to guess, I would say it was similar to one of those old Looney Tune cartoons where my eyes bulged out of my head and were three times the size they normally were.

I didn't doubt Sam was good in bed, but hearing Sam with a dirty mouth was more than I was ready for.

"Don't look so surprised," he teased. "I love eating pussy."

I watched as he lowered himself between my legs and gently pushed my panties to the side, exposing me. His touch was soft and gentle as he lightly brushed his fingers along my thighs, his mouth now mere inches away from my slit.

I leaned back on my hands, watching as he looked up at me while his tongue ran across my pussy, licking up my wetness as it slid inside. I gasped and closed my eyes, the sensation enough to make me lose it.

His hands gripped my hips as he pulled me closer to the edge of the counter while he continued to fuck me with his tongue.

Everything felt so amazing that I never wanted this to end. I reached down and grabbed his short hair, slightly digging my nails into his scalp as I teetered on the edge of climax. It would be embarrassing with how quickly I came, but I didn't care. No one had ever made my body tingle the way Sam was, and I wanted every ounce of pleasure he could give me.

His grip on my hips tightened as he pressed his lips against my clit and began to suck.

"Fuck!" I cried out, gripping his hair tighter as I tried not to fall apart. "Oh my God. Fuck."

I panted hard, completely breathless, as he continued his beautiful torture on my clit. My spine started to tingle as I felt the start of the world's best orgasm. I arched my back and let my head fall back as I cried out when waves of pleasure washed over me.

Seventeen

Sam

When I thought Avery moaning while she ate was the sexiest thing ever, I was sorely mistaken. Avery climaxing on my face was by far the sexiest thing I had ever seen or heard as she cried out in pleasure, and one time wasn't going to be enough for me.

"You coming is the most beautiful thing I've ever watched," I said, gently rubbing my thumb across her cheek.

"I'm a little embarrassed because I don't think I've ever come that hard before. I think I blacked out there for a few moments and don't even know what I was saying."

"You said *Sam is the greatest, and I will do anything he wants for the rest of my life,*" I teased with a wink.

"Hmmm. I don't know. It's a possibility. Between the lattes and now this, I might be committed to doing whatever you want if it gets me more of both."

"Trust me when I say you never have to ask for either, Avery. Giving to you brings me more happiness than you can imagine."

"Well, it's funny, I was just about to say how I was suddenly in a *giving* mood." She winked and reached for my hand as she hopped off the counter and fixed her panties.

She stood in front of me, her fingers cold on my skin as she worked the button and zipper on my jeans before pulling them down my legs.

"Avery, you don't have to—" I stopped when she lowered my boxer briefs and held my hard cock in her hand.

"I want to."

Before I could say anything else, she was on her knees with my dick in her mouth as she slowly took me to the back of her throat. I closed my eyes and wrapped my fingers in her hair, loving the way her tongue felt as she flattened it around me.

She used one hand to gently massage my balls while the other hand stroked the part of my shaft she couldn't fit in her mouth. The combination was mind-blowingly incredible, and if she didn't stop, I would be coming down her throat in a matter of seconds.

"Avery," I warned, my voice deep and gruff. "I'm going to come if you don't stop."

She pulled back slightly, still keeping my cock in her mouth as she looked up at me. Dark brown eyes locked on mine and held my gaze as she bobbed up and down on my cock, gagging a few times when I'd hit the back of her throat. She loosened her jaw and increased her grip around me as she sucked harder and faster, sending me over the edge as I shot ropes of cum down her throat.

I grunted and pinched my eyes shut as the world blurred around me from the most intense orgasm I'd ever had in my life. Once I was done, she slowly pulled away and released me before standing up and wiping the corners of her mouth.

"Fuck," I said with a heavy sigh. "That was fucking amazing, Avery."

"Thanks," she replied with a cheeky grin. "I know I said I wanted you to fuck me on this counter, but I was thinking maybe we could go to your office instead. Something about fucking the boss at his desk is super arousing to me."

I let out a low growl before picking her up and tossing her over my shoulder as I carried her to the office.

I didn't expect anyone to come in since we were closed for the day and the shop was locked, but that didn't stop me from going back up front, gathering our clothes, and then locking my office door before turning to face Avery.

She was like a walking wet dream, sitting on the edge of my desk, completely naked. I loved the curves of her body and couldn't wait to explore more of it. I stripped off my boxer briefs and grabbed a condom from my wallet before I got too distracted and forgot.

"So, office sex is your thing?" I asked, standing fully naked in front of her as she leaned back and spread her legs for me.

I stroked my cock, knowing it wouldn't take much for it to be ready again. Her eyes wandered, watching as I touched myself. I had no idea what Avery was into, but this was definitely a turn-on. Maybe if I were lucky, she'd let me watch her pleasure herself as well.

"Answer me, Avery," I said, trying to get her attention again.

"I think it is. It's the idea of doing it somewhere we're not supposed to," she replied with a smirk and a giggle. "Or maybe I could fuck my *boss* to get a raise?"

"I could see that happening," I teased, leaning in to kiss her while one hand cupped her breast and gently massaged it.

"I'm a real hard worker." She leaned forward and grabbed my cock, pushing my hand away.

I lowered my mouth and kissed my way down her neck before getting where I really wanted to be. Her nipples were already hard as I pulled one into my mouth and began sucking. She whimpered and arched her back while she continued stroking my dick.

"Only good girls get raises, Avery. Are you a good girl?"

I moved from one nipple to the other, sucking harder as I waited for her answer.

"Yes!" she cried out, her legs spreading wider.

"Are you sure about that?"

"Mmm hmmm," she whimpered. "I was a good girl and took your cock down my throat, remember?"

Just the thought of her sucking me off made my dick instantly hard again.

"I do remember. You did suck it so good. But I don't know. If you want a raise, you're going to have to work for it."

I had no idea Avery was into role-playing, but when I lowered my hand and slid a finger along her slit, I felt just how wet and turned on she was right now.

"Yes, sir. Tell me what you want me to do for it."

I inserted another finger and grinned when I felt her clench around me. Her pussy was so tight that I was going to enjoy spreading her open with my cock.

"I want you to ride me on that chair over there," I said, nodding to the one in the corner that I used whenever I had a meeting in my office. It wasn't on wheels and had no arms, so it should be more than accommodating.

She looked past me to the chair and grinned.

"Yes, sir. I take my job very seriously and am willing to put in the extra work for a raise. I won't let you down."

I helped her off of the desk before grabbing the condom and sitting on the chair. She watched as I unrolled it, pinching the tip once it was on.

"Whenever you're ready," I invited, spreading my arms as my cock jutted up to my stomach.

She licked her lips and slowly walked over, gently positioning herself over my dick before lowering herself onto it. I gripped her hips and held her in place for a moment to keep from coming again. She was so tight that I didn't want to blow my load right away.

"You okay?" I asked, noticing the slight wince on her face.

"Yeah. You're big. Really big."

"And you're tight. Really tight."

"A good combination, I'd say," she teased as she slowly allowed her body to relax as she took me all the way in.

"Fuck yeah, it is," I growled, my cock already ready to explode.

"So, I'd like to start by saying that in just a short time, I've already mastered the basic latte drinks," she said, grinding her hips as her walls clenched around me.

"You have," I agreed, straining to talk while I tried to keep it together.

"I've also done well with getting orders entered into the system correctly, and my speed has increased," she said while also increasing the speed at which she was bouncing on my cock.

"I think I've worked hard for a raise, and I would appreciate your consideration." She leaned forward, changing the position so my dick lined up against her clit while her breasts bounced heavily in my face.

She fucked me hard and fast, holding herself where she needed the friction. Her head fell back as she cried out, screaming my name as another orgasm crashed over her. Watching her fall apart had me coming right alongside her.

Eighteen
Avery

Not only had I kissed Sam tonight, I'd had sex with him.

My mind was still spinning as it tried to process everything that happened. Even with all of the craziness that I wouldn't typically have done, I didn't feel any regret about any of it. While I hadn't planned on sleeping with him, I was happy that I had. Sam was an excellent lover, and I had never had anyone bring me the amount of pleasure he had.

I took a few minutes to freshen up my makeup after cleaning up and getting dressed. By the time I was done, Sam was waiting for me in the front by the registers.

"Here," he said, extending a stack of cash to me.

"Ummm. Woah." I held up my hands and took a step back as I gave him a questioning look. "I was just playing about the whole raise thing. I thought you knew that. I wasn't actually expecting you to pay me for sex."

"I'm not," he said with a chuckle as he rubbed his finger along his jawline. "I went ahead and cashed out your bonus check for you. That way, you'll have cash tonight if you want to do some shopping for Kennedy while she's not with you."

"Oh." I snapped my mouth shut, feeling completely

embarrassed as my cheeks burned redder than Rudolph's nose. "Thank you."

I accepted the money he handed me and tucked it safely into my wallet.

"You're welcome. Besides, *if* I were to pay you for sex or give you a raise based on your *performance*, it would be far higher than five hundred dollars."

"Sam!" I exclaimed, smacking him on the chest.

"What? I know what that sweet pussy of yours is worth," he replied with a smirk as he leaned in and kissed me.

His dirty talk still sent chills up my spine.

"Have dinner with me." He held my hands in his and brought one to his lips to kiss.

"Okay. Let me call Cassidy real quick and let her know I'll be late tonight. I don't want her to start worrying."

"I hope you don't mind, but I already talked to her and told her you would take her up on the offer to keep Kennedy overnight tonight."

"You did?"

"Yeah. I hope I didn't overstep. I just really wanted to have more time with you tonight."

"You didn't," I said, though it felt weird to say it. I wasn't used to having someone else make decisions when it came to my child because Grant never bothered. Everything always fell on me to handle and coordinate, so it felt weird that Sam so easily took charge and got it situated without me having to ask.

"I know you don't get a lot of time to yourself, and yes, technically, you won't be by yourself because I'll be with you," he teased. "But I thought it might be nice for you to have a night off. Go to dinner. Do some shopping. Have more sex if you're into that sort of thing."

He winked, but the blush that spread across his cheeks was adorable.

"It's funny you should mention it because I am most certainly into that sort of thing."

He took my arm and led me to the front as we officially started our first date.

****

Dinner was good, and I was relieved that Sam didn't insist on going to a stuffy restaurant where everything on the menu cost an arm and a leg. He insisted on eating at the mall and claimed they had some of the best food in Sugarplum Falls. After stuffing myself beyond full with a cheeseburger, fries, and a shake, I could see why. Plus, there were plenty of stores to shop, which meant I'd have time to walk off some of the unnecessary calories I'd just eaten.

"Do you know what you want to get Kennedy for Christmas?" Sam asked as we browsed the toy section in one of the larger department stores.

"Honestly, I have no idea,' I replied, putting a Lego set back. "I used to always know what to get her, but this year, things feel so much harder. Not only is there a lot going on with us moving and not really having a place to call home, but as she gets older, her interests change so quickly. I feel like no matter what I get, it won't be the right thing."

"Well, first, you do have a place to call home, and you can stay there as long as you want," Sam said, pointing at me with a slight glare. "Second, it's okay that things are changing. We still have time to figure out what to get her."

"Christmas is in ten days. I've pulled shit together in the eleventh hour before, but even this feels impossible. If I wasn't so distracted with everything else, I could take the time to focus on her and what she likes these days."

"Stop being so hard on yourself," he said, gently rubbing my back. "You're her mom, and you know her better than anyone. Why don't we shop for other stuff and come back to the toys later?"

"Okay," I agreed, letting out a heavy breath as I nodded my head. "I still need to get something for Cassidy and your parents. Who all is on your list?"

"You and Kennedy," he replied with a slight grin. "So, if you could casually look around and make a big deal over the things you like, that would be a big help."

"You do not have to buy for me, Sam. Really. I appreciate the thought, but it's not necessary."

He stepped in close, pulled me against his body, and lowered his mouth to my ear.

"Do you really think I'm going to fuck you in my office and devour your pussy like it's my last meal but then *not* get you something for Christmas?"

My cheeks flushed with color as I looked around to see if anyone had heard him. Thankfully, it was relatively quiet in the store, and the few people who were there weren't close enough to hear our conversation.

Before I could answer him, my phone started ringing. I pulled it out of my pocket, and then worry rushed over me as I saw Cassidy's name.

"Hey, Cass. What's wrong?"

"Why do you assume that something's wrong?"

"Well, because you're watching my daughter and calling me, so yeah, my first guess is that something happened with Kennedy."

"Nope. She's fine. We're watching movies and having popcorn."

"Okay," I said, not bothering to comment on how late it was or that the popcorn might give her an upset stomach. "What's going on then?"

"I was calling to see if you wouldn't mind picking up a few packs of tape and a roll of wrapping paper for me while you're there."

"Oh. Yeah. Not a problem. Any certain print or color you want?"

I smiled at Sam as he mouthed *who's that.*

"It's your sister," I said, moving the phone slightly away from my mouth. "She needs tape and wrapping paper, so don't let me forget to grab some."

"Tell her to get it herself," he said with a frown.

"Tell him I said to stop being a jerk and buy it for me."

"Do you want me to put you on the phone with him?" I asked with a laugh, knowing this was just the start of them razzing each other.

"No, I'm good. I'm hanging out with Kennedy and don't have time for his nonsense. But I'm helping her finish wrapping her gifts tomorrow, but we ran out of supplies."

"What do you mean *her gifts*?"

"She might have made some stuff for everyone," Cassidy said in a tone that I immediately recognized.

"Made or bought?" I questioned with my hand on my hip.

"Both."

"Cassidy," I exhaled heavily. "You guys don't need to be giving her money to buy stuff. She's five. When I'm back on my feet, I'll start giving her allowance again, but until then, you guys don't need to do that."

"Well, first of all—I didn't give her money."

"Okay, then who did?"

"My parents."

That didn't surprise me any.

"And Sam."

My eyes widened as my head whipped around to stare at him. He winced and scrunched his shoulders, already knowing he'd been caught.

"You guys have got to be kidding me," I groaned. "I can't trust you for shit."

"Hey, that's not true. You can trust us," Cassidy argued. "It's not hurting anyone, Avery. She wanted to be a big girl and shop for people herself. We just helped make that happen."

"How is it that my five-year-old already knows what to get people and has her shopping done, yet I can't think of a single thing she wants?" I blinked quickly to try to force away the tears, but the emotion in my voice was evident.

"Oh, Avery," Cassidy whispered. "Honey, I'm so sorry. I didn't know you were struggling with that."

"Yeah, well, I haven't had much time to think about it. But now that I'm out shopping with Sam, I'm drawing blanks on what to get her. On what to get anyone." I threw my hand in the air helplessly as Sam gave me space.

"It's okay. Do you want me to go shopping with you this weekend? Frosty Fest is happening, and they always have tons of good stuff. We can make a whole day of it and take Kennedy to the parade in the morning," Cassidy offered.

"I can't buy stuff for her without her seeing if she's there with me."

"True." Cassidy took a deep breath and then blew it out.

"Okay, how about you try to do some shopping with Sam tonight? Then we can finish stuff this weekend. I'll have my parents go with us and we can distract Kennedy while you purchase stuff, then one of us can go hide it in my parent's car."

"You do realize that none of this is a secret if she's sitting right there?" I asked, feeling even more defeated.

"I went to my room for a few minutes so she didn't hear me. She's cuddled with my mom on the couch. I honestly don't think she even realizes that I'm gone."

"Okay. I'm sorry. I'm just getting frustrated. I didn't mean to take it out on you."

"Don't be. I get it."

"Thanks for helping with everything. I'll see what I can get done tonight, and then we'll plan to attack the rest this weekend."

"It'll be alright, Avery. I promise."

"You say that now, but you haven't had to shop for a five-year-old who you have no idea what they want."

"I actually already did my shopping for Kennedy," she said quietly.

"Are you kidding? How did you know what to get her?"

"I cheated," Cassidy admitted with a laugh. "I've been taking note of what toys she gets excited about when commercials come on, then I go add it to the list on my phone."

"Did you already buy everything on that list, or are there a few things you weren't able to get?" I asked, chewing my nails nervously.

"There are five or six things I didn't get. I'll take a screenshot and send it over once we hang up."

"Thanks, Cass. You're a lifesaver."

"Not a problem. If you need help with anything else, just let me know."

"Do you by chance have a similar list of things your brother wants?" I lowered my voice and turned so he couldn't hear me.

"No, but he's pretty simple. He likes graphic t-shirts, beanies, and tools that he never bothers to use."

"Is that it?" I didn't want to get Sam stuff that wasn't special, but I couldn't just come out and tell Cassidy that I spent the afternoon fucking her brother so I needed a more personal gift.

"That's all I can think of off the top of my head. Why?"

"No reason. I just want to make sure I get him something nice. You know, as a token of my gratitude for everything he's done for me lately."

The line was eerily quiet for a few seconds, and I knew she could hear the change in my voice.

"Oh my God."

"What?" I asked, playing stupid as I stared across the store, hoping she wasn't going to say what I thought she was.

"You're hooking up with my brother, aren't you?"

Nineteen

Sam

"Don't you think you're going a little overboard on stuff for Cassidy?" I said, frowning as Avery added another set of scented candles to the shopping cart.

"She's my best friend, and she's been doing a lot for me lately by helping out with Kennedy."

Avery had been acting weird ever since she hung up with my sister. Not only did she get two packs of tape and seven rolls of wrapping paper, she was adding an endless amount of crap to the shopping cart that Cassidy definitely didn't need.

She took off down the next aisle, scanning the scarf and glove sets before I stepped in and blocked her.

"Avery, stop."

She looked surprised as her eyes struggled to focus on me and not the display behind me.

"I need to finish my shopping," she insisted. "It was your idea that we did this, remember?"

"Yes. I suggested going shopping and getting stuff for Kennedy while you were able to without having to worry about hiding anything from her. What you're doing is guilt buying a ton of random shit for my sister, who doesn't need any of it."

She opened her mouth to speak but then stopped.

"Does Cassidy know about us?" I asked, stepping closer to her.

She nodded and then began chewing her lower lip.

"Okay." I stepped to the side and began grabbing stuff from the cart to put back.

"Sam! Don't! I need that stuff," she insisted, trying to block me.

"No, baby. You don't." I gently pinched her chin between my fingers to force her to look at me. "I don't care about what Cassidy thinks, and you shouldn't either. There's also no need to get her all of this stuff just because you're hooking up with her brother."

"What if she's mad at me for it?"

"Did she sound mad?"

"I don't know. Kennedy came into the room right as she said it, so she said she had to go. What if she doesn't want to be my friend anymore because of this?"

"Then she's stupid, and you deserve better friends."

"Sam, she's your sister!"

"I know. And out of everyone, I have the right to call her stupid. It's a brotherly privilege."

"That's not helping anything."

"And neither is this," I said, pointing to the shopping cart full of stuff. "Avery, if she can't be happy for you, then that's her problem. If she doesn't want to be your friend because we hooked up, that's also her problem. But there is absolutely no reason for you to spend this kind of money on trying to suck up to her. Spend it on Kennedy, and whatever you have leftover, spend that on yourself."

"I don't like people to be mad at me," she said sadly. "Especially Cassidy. She's my best friend."

"I know. And if I know my sister, she was more surprised by the news than mad. Give her some time; then you guys can talk about it."

"I'm supposed to go shopping with her this weekend at the Frosty Fest. I'm hoping we have a chance to talk before then because I don't want it to ruin the day. Do you want to come with us?"

"I wish I could, but I'll be running the Sugarplum Lattes booth there. But I'm glad you guys are going. It's really fun, and Kennedy will love the reindeer. They always have them in a pen after the parade so the kids can go feed them. Santa and Mrs. Claus will be there too, so you can take Kennedy to see them."

She nodded, but I could still see the wheels in her mind going a mile a minute. I took the opportunity while she was distracted and started putting most of the stuff she'd picked for Cassidy back.

"What else did you want to look for in here?" I asked, taking over steering the shopping cart.

"Cassidy sent me a list with a few things she said Kennedy wanted. I guess she's been making notes of the stuff Kennedy sees on TV and wants, which is better than anything I've got. She finished her shopping, so she said these items were good to buy."

"Can I see the list?" I asked, pulling to the side of the aisle so we were out of the way.

"Sure." She handed her phone to me, and I cringed when I saw the list.

"What?" she demanded, her shoulders slumping and disappointment heavy in her voice. "You already bought these for her, didn't you?"

"Maybe." I shrugged and offered her a smile, hoping she still found it somewhat cute.

"I am never going to get my shopping for her done," she groaned, closing her eyes.

"I'm so sorry. I honestly didn't even think about it. I just noticed she seemed so excited when she saw them, so I had to grab them."

"It's okay." She sighed heavily and looked into the shopping cart that was now almost empty. "Maybe I should just give up for tonight and try again this weekend. This isn't going quite as I had hoped."

"That's not a terrible idea," I said, keeping my tone gentle. "Maybe tomorrow night we can sit down and help her write her list to Santa. Unless she's already done that?"

"Oh my God," Avery groaned, putting her hand to her head. "I completely forgot about the damn list until now. I'm a terrible mother."

"You're not a terrible mother. You're an overwhelmed human who has a lot on her plate right now. But we can handle this, okay? Let's go pay for what we have, and then we'll work on getting a list out of her tomorrow. We can go from there, and I can even send you to run errands while I watch Kennedy so you can sneak out and buy stuff."

She took a deep breath in and slowly released it.

"Okay. We can make that work."

I smiled and wrapped an arm around her shoulder as we walked to the front registers to pay for what we had.

"You're really good at this," she commented vaguely.

"Shopping?"

"No. Parenting. You're going to make a wonderful husband and father someday."

<u>Twenty</u>

Avery

"Isn't it too late to make a list for Santa?" Kennedy questioned with a frown on her face. "Christmas is in one week."

"It's never too late, sweetie," I assured her, hoping she didn't hear the crack in my voice. I didn't know if she was able to remember when we usually did our letters to Santa, but I hoped that she was young enough for it to be super vague in her memories.

"I don't even know what I want."

I could feel my blood pressure start to rise, worried this was a terrible idea after all. Sam rested his hand on my shoulder reassuringly, and it instantly calmed my nerves.

He pulled out the chair on the other side of Kennedy and sat down.

"I always had a hard time writing my list to Santa when I was little," he said, pulling Kennedy's attention to him.

"You did?"

He nodded.

"Yeah. I didn't want to ask for anything too big because I was worried it would never fit in the sleigh. And then I would worry that if I picked a gift that was too big, then there wouldn't be room in his sack for gifts for other kids. So then I would try to think of small gifts but would worry that if they were too small, they'd get lost, and he wouldn't know he had a gift for me."

"I didn't even think about that," Kennedy said with wide eyes.

"Well, the thing is that I used to overthink everything. Then, one day, my mom and dad sat down with me to write my letter, and they reminded me of the most important thing about gifts from Santa."

"What's that?"

"That they always have magic."

Her eyes widened as a smile ghosted her lips.

"Magic?"

He grinned and nodded again.

"Magic was the key to getting what I wanted for Christmas because then I didn't have to worry if it was too big or too small. Santa would use his magic to make sure the gift made its way under the tree."

"Wow. That's so cool. What was your favorite gift you got from Santa?"

He leaned back in his chair and scratched at the stubble of his five o'clock shadow.

"Hmmm. That's a tough one. I think my favorite gift from Santa was my chemistry set. I was obsessed with knowing how and why things worked, so it was a lot of fun for me to do different experiments and see what happened."

"Did things explode?!"

"Sometimes," he admitted with a laugh. "But nothing serious or dangerous. My dad helped me with a lot of it, which is why I think it's one of my favorite gifts. It brought me a lot of happy memories with my dad."

"I don't have happy memories with mine," Kennedy said, lowering her head.

My heart exploded in my chest as a wave of emotions rushed over me. This was the first time Kennedy had ever said that out loud. Grant wasn't around much when she got older and didn't really bother to try to bond with her when she was a baby. He wasn't abusive to her, other than withholding affection and not giving her any attention. But to hear her say that she didn't have any happy memories with him broke my heart. It wasn't that I wanted Grant to step up and be the best dad for her; it was that I wanted her to have someone who *wanted* to be a good dad to her.

"I'm sorry. That has to be hard," Sam said empathetically. "I had a friend growing up that his parents got divorced when he was little, and it was really hard on him."

"What did he do?"

"He learned to adjust to all of the changes, but he was lucky that he had parents who loved him and tried to make things as easy as possible for him."

"I don't think my dad loved me," Kennedy said with a sniffle.

I turned my head to keep her from seeing the tears in my eyes. I knew this day would come, but I wasn't ready for it to happen now.

"Do you know what I think?" Sam said, continuing the conversation since I couldn't.

"What?"

"I think your dad loved you in the best way he knew how. Sometimes that might not be easy for us to see or feel, especially if we're used to feeling loved in different ways. But I don't think your dad *didn't* love you. I think he just didn't know how to show you."

"Oh. Maybe he should have asked Mommy for help. She always tells me she loves me and gives the best hugs."

"Yeah, maybe. But sometimes people have to learn to love themselves before they can learn how to love others the way they need."

I wiped my eyes and tried to pull myself together.

"Okay, so now that we know about Santa's magic, did you think of anything you want to add to your list?" Sam asked, completely changing the subject.

I got up and blew my nose, making sure I had it together before I sat down at the table again.

"I really want this art set," Kennedy said, taking us both by surprise. "I saw it on Grandma Amelia's table, and she let me see all of the pretty paint colors inside."

My heart felt like it was going to melt again as I smiled down at my beautiful daughter. I didn't even bother to correct her on calling Amelia *grandma* because if that's what she felt like she was to her, so be it. It wasn't like we had a relationship with my parents, and now Grant's were out of the picture, too.

"I think that's an excellent thing to put on the list. Are there other art supplies you think you might want to add as well?"

"Oh! Aunt Cassidy has these fun scissors that make weird lines when you cut with them. Some go this way, and some go that way." She moved her finger in the air to show us the zigzag patterns she was talking about.

"Awesome! Let's add those as well."

I felt the tension start to lift from my shoulders as the spirit in my daughter came back to life. I knew I'd been in a funk and battling depression the past few months with all of the changes, but I never stopped to think about how much it was affecting Kennedy. I was thankful for a lot these days, but tonight, I was most grateful for the friends who had quickly become family and were helping us through these challenging times.

Twenty-One

Sam

After Avery got Kennedy down for the night, she came and joined me on the couch. I had made her a cup of warm tea, knowing that she needed it tonight.

"Thank you for your help with getting Kennedy's list done," she said, curling into the side of me as she took a sip. "And thank you for the tea."

"My pleasure on both."

"Do you think it would be rude to ask your mom where she got the art set Kennedy was talking about?"

"Not at all. But my guess is that she bought her one the second she saw her interest in hers. My mom is quick like that."

"Well, I guess we better ask before I buy anything from the list. At least we have a good range of things to work off of now. Between the arts and crafts stuff and the toys, I feel like we made some good progress."

"That we did." I kissed the top of her head, enjoying her being so close to me.

"And thank you for your help with the conversation about her dad." Avery leaned forward and set her cup on the coffee table before turning to face me. "I didn't see that coming, and unfortunately, I wasn't prepared for it. So thank you for stepping in when I couldn't handle it."

"Avery, you don't have to thank me. I'd like to think that we're doing things as a team right now, and that's what teammates do—they help each other out. It's okay that you didn't know how to handle it because it wasn't an easy thing to handle. Not only that, but it's impossible for you to know how to react to her emotions when yours are tied so heavily to it. Not only do you feel for her as a mother, but you have your own feelings tied to her relationship with her father. It's a hard situation, and no one expects that you have it all figured out."

"Thank you. I knew that eventually we'd need to talk about her feelings toward her father. I just didn't think it would happen so soon. He's been out of her life for so long, I'm surprised she even acknowledged his absence."

"Was he not there much when she was growing up?" I knew some of the details that she'd given me in random conversations, but I felt the need to know more.

"He traveled for work a lot, and by travel, he was secretly living another life with his mistress. When he was home, he spent a lot of time in his office or zoned out in front of the TV. I gave up on trying to force him to have a relationship with Kennedy once I found out about the affair."

"Wow. That sucks." I couldn't imagine being that big of an asshole and ruining my family.

"It does, but sometimes I think it was easier to walk away from everything because he never bothered to have that bond with her. When we separated, he made it clear that he had no interest in having custody of her. He always said he wasn't sure if he wanted kids. I should have known then that he would be a shitty father. As much as I hate him, I'm thankful that he gave me Kennedy. She's the best thing that's ever happened to me."

"She's the best thing that happened to all of us," I said softly, pulling her closer to me. "I know I'm not supposed to, but I love her, Avery. I love her like I would love my own child, and it kills me that she feels her father doesn't love her. I would replace that love for her in a heartbeat if I were able to."

I could feel her body stiffen beneath me and worried that I had said too much and overstepped another boundary. But then I heard her sniffle and felt the warm tear as it fell on my arm and I knew that she was trying to hide her emotions from me again.

"I don't know if I'm supposed to say that or not, but I mean it. I would go to the ends of the earth to make her happy. To make both of you happy. He's an asshole who isn't worthy of either of your love and as bad as it is to say it, I'm happy he's out of the picture. You both deserve so much more than that. You deserve the world and all of the happiness there is to give."

"I don't know how I got so lucky to find someone like you," she said, sniffling before lifting her lips to mine.

I'm sure it was meant to be an innocent kiss, but nothing with me and Avery stayed innocent for long these days.

Within minutes, we had gone from a calm, gentle kiss to her straddling me on the couch and making out. We were both so distracted that neither of us heard the little footsteps as they padded down the hallway and into the living room.

"Mommy? What are you doing to Uncle Sam?"

Twenty-Two
Avery

"Honey!" I exclaimed, jumping off Sam quicker than a bucking bronco in the rodeo.

Kennedy rubbed her eyes and frowned.

"Were you two kissing?"

I rubbed my lips together as I tugged my shirt down, hoping she hadn't seen his hand up it as he fondled my breast.

"Umm," I said, hesitating to answer.

"Yeah, we were," Sam answered coolly.

I gave him an angry look and swatted his chest before climbing off the couch and rushing over to her.

"What? Why bother lying to her when she clearly saw us? She's not stupid," he said quietly for only me to hear.

I knew that she had seen us, but that didn't mean I wasn't going to live in denial for as long as possible. Admitting it only forced it to be more real, and I wasn't ready to explain whatever this thing between him and I was to her yet.

"Honey, what's wrong? Why are you up?"

"I had a bad dream."

"I'm sorry. Do you want to tell me what it was about while we go lie down in your bed?"

She shook her head, and tears filled her eyes.

"Oh, honey," I said, pulling her into me for a hug. "Whatever it was, it was just a dream. I promise."

"I want Sam to tuck me in. He's the only one who can protect me!"

I pressed a hand to my heart and frowned, wondering what in the world could have upset her so badly. Within an instant, Sam was off the couch and headed right for her.

"What happened in your dream, sweetheart?" he asked, concern heavy on his face.

"A monster came and tried to take me from my mommy," she said, crying hard as she let him pick her up and hold her.

I was torn between feeling an endless amount of love toward this man who was comforting my daughter right now and jealousy that she had picked him over me. For five beautiful years, I had always been the one she went to.

"Monsters aren't real, honey. No one can take you from me," I assured her as I rubbed her back while she laid her head on Sam's chest.

"It wasn't a real monster," she cried. "It was daddy."

I turned away and waved my hand in front of my eyes to keep them from letting out the tears that were begging to be set free.

I knew Sam was right behind me because of the way my

body instantly reacted. But I couldn't deal with that right now. My world felt like it was crumbling around me, and it was taking everything in me to try to stay standing.

"I think we should talk about this," Sam said, placing his hand on my shoulder.

I nodded and sucked in another deep breath, struggling to keep it together.

"Yes. You're right. We should talk about it. That's a great idea." I smiled and wiped the tears from Kennedy's face as I followed Sam to the couch and sat beside them.

Kennedy stayed glued to his side like a little baby koala, too afraid to let go. I took a moment to lock the memory of him holding her right now into my heart because this was something I would never want to forget.

"I know your dream must have felt really scary, sweetie," Sam started, making eye contact with Kennedy as she barely lifted her head to see him. "But I promise, no one will ever take you from your mommy."

"How do you know? What if my dad comes back and tries to take me just to hurt Mommy?"

"Even if he did, he would have to get through me first."

"And he can't do that because you're strong?"

"The strongest."

"And you protect me and Mommy?"

"Always and forever."

"And even if daddy came back, you would stop him?"

"If your daddy ever came back, your mom would take care of things. There are a lot of things that are for adults to worry about, and this would be one of them. But no matter what, I would be there to take care of your mommy."

"And the baby?"

I leaned forward and frowned, confused about this turn of events.

"What baby?" I asked.

"The baby in your tummy. Uncle Sam's baby. You guys would protect that baby too, right?"

I felt all of the color drain from my face. This was too much. Way too much to process or deal with right now.

She had just barely seen us kissing a few minutes ago, so why was she having a dream that I was carrying his child?

Twenty-Three

Avery

"She what?" Cassidy hissed as we walked through the Frosty Fest sipping lattes. Kennedy walked in front of us, snuggled between Amelia and Ron as she held their hands and swung them high in the air.

"She said that Sam was going to have to protect us from Grant and then went on to mention *Uncle Sam's baby* in my tummy."

"Are you?"

"No!" I blurted out, still feeling out of sorts and overwhelmed by everything. "We only had sex one time, and we used a condom. So unless the universe is messing with me and it was defective, we should be fine."

"I bet the baby will look like me," Cassidy replied, completely ignoring my current freak-out.

"Could you not make this about you right now?"

"Oh, calm down. It's probably nothing. I mean, I am still a bit shocked that you and my brother are hooking up, but I can't say that I didn't see it coming."

"What are you talking about?"

"I'm talking about how you two have liked each other for

years, and the second you came back to town he looked like one of those idiots in the movies with the stars in his eyes. I knew it was only a matter of time before you guys acted on it, especially once you moved in with him."

"I did not move in with him. We're just staying there temporarily."

"I don't know that Kennedy will love sharing her room with a baby. You guys might want to start looking for a new house. One with more space for your growing family."

"You're the worst," I joked, taking a sip of my latte as I followed Kennedy to a booth with stuffed animals. "Also— if you buy her another stuffie, I will permanently disown you."

"Yikes. Someone is wound up today," Sam joked, startling me as he snuck up behind me. "But I don't blame you. Cassidy will do that to people."

"Hey," I said, turning to give him a kiss.

Once we came clean to Kennedy, she took the privilege of telling everyone she knew that Mommy and Uncle Sam were dating. It was kind of nice not to have to worry about our relationship in public, but I definitely felt like people at work were judging me.

"She's just grumpy because Kennedy won't stop trying to tell people about your *little secret*," Cassidy said loudly behind her hand.

Sam looked at me and frowned. I shook my head and let out an irritated breath.

"She thinks that Kennedy's dream is real, and she's getting a little too excited about *something* that's not even on *the way*."

Amelia and Ron turned to give us a curious glance but then had their attention pulled away by Kennedy, who was showing them the Santa and Mrs. Claus stuffies. I knew it was only a matter of time before someone pulled out their wallet and bought them for her.

"I mean, if that's what she wants, I don't mind leaving work early and going home to make that dream a reality," Sam offered, tickling my sides.

"Oh my gosh," I said with a snort. "You two knock it off. I can't handle both of you right now."

"No, but you sure can handle this cock tonight when we're alone," Sam whispered in my ear, giving me chills.

"Eeeew. Stop." Cassidy dramatically shivered as if she had any idea what her brother just said to me.

"You don't even know what he said," I objected, swatting her on the arm.

"No, but it's the way he's looking at you. Get a room already."

"We have one. At my house. Which will be empty tonight while we wrap presents and have—"

"Don't you dare," I warned, knowing Kennedy was eavesdropping again. It was her new favorite thing, and I found we had to be even more careful about what we said these days.

"Fine, take all the fun away. I gotta get back to the booth, but I just thought I'd come say hi. Let me know when you're done, and I'll see if I can get out early."

"Okay, I will."

I leaned up and kissed him on the cheek, feeling nervous about PDA in front of his parents. He chuckled and smacked me on the ass when no one was looking, making my skin flush with heat.

I tried to stay focused on what Kennedy was looking at so I could finish the rest of my shopping. Thankfully, I had already bought things for Cassidy, Amelia, and Ron, but I wanted to make sure Kennedy had plenty to open on Christmas morning.

It was our first Christmas without her dad, and while I knew she was feeling angry toward him, I didn't know how she would feel Christmas morning with everything being different. I hated that I couldn't give her the familiarity of doing Christmas in the house she grew up in, but deep down, I hoped that these new experiences would be enough to shape some happy memories for her.

I sent Kennedy off with Cassidy for a bit while I made my way back around to all of the booths we could keep track of and bought the last gifts for Kennedy. Amelia and Ron were champions at remembering exactly which items she wanted and went out of their way to take the shopping bags to their car so she didn't see them.

By the time we were done, I was exhausted and ready to call it a day.

I texted Sam to let him know we were finishing up and that I would get a ride back to his place with his parents since they were dropping off all of the gifts we were hiding from Kennedy.

He replied to let me know he would grab takeout on his way home and that he was leaving soon. The plan was to have dinner, drink some wine, and then put on Christmas music while we spent the night wrapping all of our gifts together—minus the ones we got for each other. It was weird how we fell so easily into a relationship and how my heart was so open to it. I'd felt a happiness with Sam that I hadn't ever felt with anyone before, including Grant.

138

Twenty-Four

Sam

"How's your chicken lo mein?" I asked Avery as I popped a piece of orange chicken into my mouth and chewed.

"It's delicious. You should try it." She leaned over on the couch and held her hand beneath the noodles she'd twirled around her fork as she held it out for me.

I took the bite and closed my eyes, savoring the flavor as it hit my tongue.

"That is good," I said, wiping my mouth as I finished chewing. "Do you want some orange chicken?"

"Sure." She grinned and waited for me to feed her and I couldn't get over how incredible it felt to be having moments like this with Avery.

"Oh my gosh," she moaned, making my dick twitch. "That's delicious, too."

"I think it's safe to say that everything they make there is going to be five-star. I don't think I've ever gotten food from them I didn't like."

"Well, they might be my new go-to when I don't feel like cooking. I bet Kennedy would love it, too."

"Does that mean you're planning to stay in Sugarplum Falls for good?" I asked with a little too much hope in my voice.

"Honestly? I haven't decided. When I was little, I kept telling myself that someday I would grow up and move away to a big city where the opportunities would be endless. When I had Kennedy, I always felt that I wanted the same for her. But being back in Sugarplum Falls, it's kinda nice not having the rush of a big city, even if everyone knows your business all the time."

"I know big cities have their appeal, but where else can you go that has a hot barista that makes the *best* gingerbread lattes?" I teased with a wink.

"You have a point," she replied with a giggle. "But it's hard because it's not just me I have to worry about. I have to think ahead to the future and what might be best for Kennedy. I want to make sure that I give her everything I can and that I set her up for whatever path she decides to go down. Sometimes, I worry that I will limit her if we stay here."

"I get that, and I can't imagine how stressful it is being a parent and having to make those kinds of decisions. And while I'm not trying to sway you to stay, I think it's important to note how many incredibly successful people have come from Sugarplum Falls. Some have moved and travel across the world for work, while others have built their empires here. Kennedy is an incredibly smart little girl with a momma who will move mountains to give her what she needs. I think she's going to be more than fine, no matter what path you choose."

Avery smiled, but I could see the way my words weighed heavily on her mind.

Once we finished dinner, I poured each of us a glass of wine and grabbed the supplies so we could start wrapping presents. Avery came out of her bedroom with shopping bags lined up on each arm and grinned when she saw the pile I'd already set out.

"Do you think we went a little overboard?" she asked, chewing her lip as she added her bags to the pile.

"No. There's no such thing as going overboard when Kennedy is involved."

Her face softened as she gave me the sweetest smile. I wasn't lying when I told her that I loved Kennedy like she was my own child. It didn't take long before she'd worked her way into my heart and I knew I would do whatever it took to make that little girl happy.

"I don't even know where to start," Avery admitted, looking around the room.

"Well, find a spot and get comfy. We'll dive in from there."

She sat in front of the couch and leaned against it as I handed her scissors, several rolls of tape, and wrapping paper. I grabbed the bags my parents had dropped off earlier from Frosty Fest and decided we would start there.

"Have you decided which gift is from Santa?" I asked, looking through the other rolls of wrapping paper to find the one I was looking for.

"I think I'm going to go with the dollhouse that she asked for today when she sat on his lap. I had no idea she wanted one, but Cassidy made it her mission to find one at Waldon's before they sold out. I guess it's convenient she works there and was able to pull some strings. It should be that big box over there," she said, pointing to the one in the corner with a bag pulled down over it.

I walked over and grabbed it, surprised by how heavy it was.

"So, the gift from Santa—is it wrapped and left under the tree, or do you assemble it and leave it out for her to find in the morning in front of the tree?" I asked, not remembering how my parents used to do it.

"I've always wrapped them and put them under the tree with the other gifts. I recently saw a post on social media where they assembled the gifts and left them out in front of the tree, but I kinda like her getting to open it instead."

"Sounds good to me. Did you want to assemble everything first so she can play with it right away?"

"Oh yeah. Definitely. I learned the hard way early on about how impatient kids are on Christmas morning. Now I make sure everything is out of its packaging and batteries are installed if it needs them."

"That's smart. I like the way you think."

I opened the box and started pulling pieces out when Avery came over to help me. It was like we were parents, tag-teaming Christmas duties to make sure our child had the best Christmas ever.

There was far more assembly than I would have imagined, and I didn't even bother to ask how much Cassidy had spent on the doll house. I knew her employee discount helped, but it still had to cost a pretty penny. It was three stories with an elevator in the middle and tons of little furniture to go inside. It also came with the cutest family, which included a mom, a dad, a little girl, and a baby swaddled in a blanket.

"She's going to love this," Avery said, stepping back to look at it once it was complete.

"Yeah, she is. I mean, I love it and I'm not a five-year-old little girl," I joked, though I seriously hoped Kennedy would let me play with it with her.

Now that it's built, I don't know how we're going to wrap it," Avery noted, chewing her nails.

"We can put it back in the box carefully, then wrap the box."

"Do you think it will fit? It looks too big."

I scrunched my face and grabbed the box, holding it beside the house.

"You're right. It's too big."

She pulled her mouth to the side as she contemplated.

"We could cut the box and make a bigger one that covers the top half of the house," I offered. "Then that would allow us something to attach the wrapping paper to. As long as the paper goes to the bottom, it won't matter if there's a box there since it'll still cover it. We'll just have to be careful moving it."

"That could work. Do you want to wait until we're done wrapping everything else? We might have a few more boxes that are trash that we can use and MacGyver them into one big box."

"Yeah. Let's do that. We can save this one for last. The nice thing is that it's already built, so we know how big it is."

She nodded her head and then looked at the pile of gifts we still had to wrap.

"It's going to be a long night," she said, grabbing her glass of wine from the coffee table and taking a sip.

"Yeah, but it'll be fun."

She rolled her eyes playfully, but there was nothing more I wanted to do right now than spend time with her—even if we were up to our elbows in gifts to wrap.

Twenty-Five
Avery

My body was sore by the time Sam and I finished wrapping gifts. The pile looked endless when we first started, but thankfully, it went quickly, with both of us working on it together. A lot of it was for Kennedy, but we also tackled wrapping our gifts for the rest of his family.

I still had a pile of stuff hidden in my room that I needed to wrap for Sam, but that would have to wait until I was by myself so he didn't see them. I could always have Kennedy help me this week while Sam was at work, as long as she promised not to tell him what we'd gotten him. She loved secrets and surprising people, but lately, she had been terrible at keeping them. It was as if she got too excited and couldn't hold it in anymore.

The tree looked amazing, lit up with all of the presents tucked beneath it. It made my heart happy that I was able to pull things together to make sure Kennedy had a good Christmas. Aside from what felt like an endless amount of toys she was getting, I'd also spent a good chunk of money buying her new clothes for the winter since she'd gone through another growth spurt recently. The bonus check from Sam had been spent quickly, but it was so incredibly appreciated and needed.

When we left North Carolina, we didn't take much with us.

Kennedy had already outgrown the baby toys she had when she was little, and I hadn't been able to afford to get her many age-appropriate toys due to trying to make ends meet the past few years. We'd brought the few toys she had, which she never complained about. That was why it made me so happy to be able to spoil her with so many new toys this year.

Even though I had no clue where we were going or what we were doing, it felt like a blessing that I was able to focus on her right now and not everything else that continuously stressed me. I had a job and thanks to Sam, a place to live without having to worry about paying rent—even though I'd offered to help out several times.

"You ready for bed?" he asked, coming up behind me and slipping a hand around my waist as he kissed my shoulder.

"Yeah. I'm exhausted. I can't believe how many gifts there are under the tree."

"I know. And just think, there will be even more because I haven't wrapped yours yet."

I turned my head to look at him over my shoulder.

"I told you that you didn't need to get me anything, Sam."

"And I told you I was going to. You can't stop me from doing something I want to do, Avery."

"Fine. I guess we'll add yours under the tree along with mine that I still need to wrap for you."

He spun me around so fast that I nearly lost my balance before he steadied me with his hand.

"Avery, I told you not to buy for me."

"Yeah, and I told you the same. But yet here we are."

"It's different. I can—"

He stopped, nearly choking on his words before he said them.

"Afford it?" I offered, tilting my head.

"That's not how I meant it."

"I know. But it's the truth."

"Things are just different. You have a child to buy for. That's where your money should go, Avery. Not on stuff for me."

"Well, I did spend money on her. A lot of it thanks to the generous bonus I got. But I also had enough to get for those I love…"

It was my turn to let the words die on my tongue as I said them. I rubbed my lips together and quickly tried to look away before his fingers grabbed my chin and redirected me to look at him.

"I'm sorry, what was that?" he asked, the grin on his face matching the humor in his eyes.

"Nothing. I just meant that I bought gifts for people in my life who I like very much."

"Stop lying to me."

"Fine," I said, widening my eyes and blowing out a breath. "Love. For people I *love*."

"You love me?" He pulled his lower lip between his teeth, still grinning at me.

I could feel the heat from his body as he pulled me closer.

"Yes, Sam. I love you. There, are you happy?"

"Happier than you could ever know. I love you too, Avery."

His smile was contagious as I started grinning back at him.

He pulled me tighter as his lips feathered over mine.

"Since Kennedy is having a sleepover tonight, would you like to have a sleepover with me in my bed?" he offered.

"Are you asking me to sleep with you?" I teased, narrowing my eyes at him.

"Yes."

"As in have sex with you or as in actually sleep with you?"

"Both."

I giggled as he bent down and tossed me over his shoulder, carrying me to his room.

We'd only had sex once, and while it was hot, it was also rushed and in his office. Having the entire house to ourselves without having to worry about any interruptions would be pure heaven.

Twenty-Six
Sam

Hearing Avery say that she loved me was something I wanted to hear over and over. It melted my heart and soothed my soul in a way I had never felt before and I hated the lingering thought in my head that it might be short-lived if she decided to leave Sugarplum Falls.

She'd slept in my bed the entire night, and unfortunately, we were both too exhausted to do anything but sleep.

I got up early and started breakfast, not sure what time Kennedy would be back. It was crazy, but I had already missed her, and she hadn't even been gone for an entire day. Another reason I couldn't stand the thought of them leaving. How would I be able to go on with life knowing that the weight of their loss would absolutely consume me?

"Good morning," Avery said as she came into the kitchen wearing nothing but one of my t-shirts.

"Good morning, indeed," I replied, pulling her into me for a kiss. "But if you don't go put real clothes on, I'll have no choice but to devour you right here on this kitchen island and burn breakfast."

"I'm not that hungry," she said coyly, tugging the bottom of the shirt up. I reached back to pull it down and groaned when I felt her bare ass cheek.

"You're killing me," I groaned, closing my eyes and taking a deep breath. "Kennedy will be back any second, and I'm going to have to go hide in the bathroom until this stupid erection goes away."

"Well, I hate to tell you this, but Cassidy just called and said your parents asked if they can keep Kennedy for the day. Apparently, she was working on some handmade Christmas gifts last night and didn't get to finish. Cassidy has to work today, but she said she can bring Kennedy back tonight after dinner."

"So I get you all to myself today?"

"It appears that way."

I reached over and turned off the stove before removing the pan from the burner.

"What are you doing?" she asked, giggling when I started putting the rest of the food stuff back in the fridge. "I'm hungry."

"Me too," I said with a playful growl. I grabbed a piece of toast from the plate and handed it to her. "Here, start with this."

"Sam! What in the world is going on?"

I picked her up and set her on the kitchen island.

"I'm hungry and having breakfast," I answered with a shrug.

"What am I supposed to do with the toast?" she asked, holding it up as she leaned back on her hand.

"You eat that while I eat you. Once we're done, I'll take you somewhere for a real breakfast."

"Sam," she said, giggling harder when I lifted the shirt over her head and tossed it to the floor. I pulled her closer to the edge of the counter, making sure she was exactly where I wanted her.

She laughed for a moment until she felt my tongue slide along her slit. She hissed out a breath as I focused on holding her in place as I played with her pussy. I loved the way she tasted as much as I loved how tight she was. We didn't have much time to play and explore each other's bodies the first time we had sex, so I was determined to find out all of the things she loved now that I had the time.

I reached for the candy cane I had opened earlier and sucked on it until it was nice and wet. Making sure there weren't any sharp or jagged ends, I slowly teased her pussy with it, tracing along her slit before slowly sliding it inside.

"What was that?" she asked, leaning forward to try to see.

"A candy cane," I replied with a grin.

"Sam!" she shrieked with a laugh. "You stuck a candy cane inside of me?"

"I sure did. A cherry one to go with your sweet pussy."

"You're going to make me all sticky," she objected, still laughing.

"Don't worry. I know how to clean you up."

I slowly twirled the candy cane around, making sure to coat her walls and clit with it the best I could before pulling it out. Then I leaned in, gripped her hips, and pressed my face against her pussy. I took my time licking every inch of her skin, making sure to get it off while enjoying the intoxicating flavor of Avery combined with the sweetness of the candy cane.

Once I was sure I had gotten it off everywhere I could, I focused my mouth on her clit and started sucking hard and fast, bringing her right to the edge.

"Oh my God, Sam," she cried out, digging her nails into my shoulders. "Fuck!"

I adjusted myself enough to be able to slide a finger inside of her without breaking the suction I currently had against her clit. She squirmed and whimpered when I added a second finger and curved them so they hit her G-spot.

"Shit!" she exclaimed, nearly knocking me over as she jolted. "Oh my God. That feels incredible."

She moaned and dug her fingers into my skin as her back arched. I increased the pressure against her G-spot, fingering her in a continuous motion as I felt her muscles start to tighten around me.

"Oh my God!" she cried out, her pussy spasming as I felt a rush of fluid on my fingers.

Once I drained every last bit out of her, I pulled back and grinned at the beautiful woman in front of me, flushed and full of color after having an incredibly intense orgasm.

Twenty-Seven
Avery

Shower sex with Sam was fun, and he wasn't lying when he said he would clean me up after fucking me with a candy cane. Also—who in the world would have ever thought a candy cane could be so erotic? At first, I was a bit worried it was a peppermint one because—woah. But thankfully, he was considerate and used a cherry one instead.

Not only did he fully eat me out after fucking me with said candy cane, he also went down on me again in the shower—just to make sure I was extra clean. When he said he loved eating pussy, he wasn't lying.

We got ready and went on our second official date, which still felt weird to say. It was pointless to deny how much I loved him, especially after I accidentally confessed it to him. If anything, it just made things harder and more complicated as I struggled to figure out my next steps. Just because we had said we loved each other and were officially dating didn't mean that I expected things to continue how they were. He invited me and Kennedy to stay with him until we got on our feet, but that didn't mean he was necessarily ready for us to live with him forever and become an instant family.

The waitress came by to refill our glasses of water while we waited for our food. Sam and I were seated in one of the booths in the back of the small café, but I could still feel people's eyes on us.

"They're still talking about us," I said quietly, trying to look away from the two older women who made no effort to hide the fact that they were indeed talking about us.

Sam looked over his shoulder and shook his head.

"People in small towns like to gossip. Give it a little time, and it'll blow over."

"How can you blow it off so easily?"

He shrugged and gave me a soft smile.

"I don't know. I guess I'm just used to it."

"You're used to being the center of the town's gossip?" I questioned, lifting my glass and taking a drink.

"No, I'm just used to the town constantly gossiping."

I must've made a weird face because his face fell and he started fidgeting with his silverware on the table.

"You're going to have people who gossip anywhere you go, Avery. Whether it's in a small town or a big city, that's just the nature of people. But you'll find here that while some people love to gossip, the majority of the town ignores it and moves on with their day. Those two live for gossip, and everyone knows that. That's why they gossip to each other; no one wants to hear it anymore."

I sighed heavily, letting my shoulders fall.

"I feel like everyone thinks that I started sleeping with you to get something at work," I admitted, twisting my napkin on my lap beneath the table.

"They can think what they want."

"It's not that easy for me, Sam. I don't want everyone thinking I'm some adulterous whore," I whispered, leaning forward so he could hear me without drawing the attention of those around us.

"No one thinks that," he said, reaching across the table for my hand.

I brought it up to the table and held his, still not believing him.

"They do," I replied, nodding to the old women who were blatantly pointing at me.

Sam got up, scooted in beside me in the booth, and stared right back at them as he talked.

"Margaret slept with her daughter's husband while her daughter was seven months pregnant with his child. She also slept with her sister's husband, leading to their divorce. Ellen, the one with the ugly beanie, got kicked out of the retirement community center because she wouldn't stop sleeping with the men there."

"Isn't that their fault, too, though?"

"Technically, yes. But she had gonorrhea and spread it like a wildfire. Sugarplum Falls had their first official outbreak of a disease that year."

"Oh my gosh!" I whispered, laughing behind my hands.

Sam turned and faced me with pure adoration in his eyes.

"You're not an adulterous whore, Avery. You're a beautiful, single woman who fell in love with the town's most eligible bachelor—who happens to make the *best* lattes, if I do say so myself. You can't blame people for being upset that you took this stud off the market."

"You're so humble," I teased, nudging him with my elbow.

I knew he was being silly just to get me to laugh, and it worked.

"You know you like it."

"Correction," I said, pausing for our waitress to deliver our food before thanking her and continuing. "I love it."

He leaned in and kissed me with more passion than was probably appropriate in public, but I didn't mind. For Sam, I would let the town continue to think I was an adulterous whore if it meant I got to be with him.

Twenty-Eight
Sam

I was disappointed when my day with Avery got cut short after I got called in to deal with another espresso-related emergency at work. I knew Piper felt bad for calling me in, but it was six days until Christmas, and people were a little crazed right now and needed their fix.

By the time we got things situated, it was already closing time so I stayed and helped. Avery texted me that Cassidy was on her way over with Kennedy. I couldn't help the excitement I felt about her coming home—even if Avery still refused to call it that.

I knew she was apprehensive about staying in Sugarplum Falls, but with each day that passed, I could see the town growing on her more and more. While I wanted what was best for Avery and Kennedy, I couldn't stop selfishly wishing that it meant they stayed and that things continued the way they were. While I had never expected to have them live with me, it just felt right now that we'd gotten into our routine. Thinking of going back to a house without them in it left a burning pain in my chest that I couldn't stand.

Just as I was locking up, I turned and found Aiden heading my way.

"Hey, did you need coffee?" I asked, wondering if he was trying to get there before we closed.

"Yes, but I'll stop somewhere else. You don't have to open for me."

"It's not a big deal," I said, unlocking the door and nodding for him to go inside.

"Is the espresso machine working again?"

"Yeah, for the most part. I ordered a new one that should be here in a few days. I was hoping to have it earlier, but that storm really messed with the roads, so there were delays. Do you want your usual?"

"Yes, please. We're doing karaoke tonight, and Jackie decided to offer a drink special with .99 Grinch shots, so I gotta be awake and functional since it's going to be packed and busy all night."

"Sounds fun," I said with a laugh.

"Are you coming?"

I started the espresso machine and hated the feeling in my stomach when I thought about missing time with Avery and Kennedy to go hang out with Aiden.

"Not tonight. I'm sorry."

"Don't be. You're fine."

"No, really. I am sorry. I've been a shitty friend lately and haven't been by in forever."

"Well, we thought for a moment we would have to close Sugar Faced Bar down after our top patron stopped coming in," Aiden teased.

I rolled my eyes and started a small pot of coffee before texting Avery to let her know I would be home a little late.

"You know how busy this time of year gets around here," I said with my back to him, not wanting him to see the lie sitting on my lips.

"Yeah. It definitely gets busy when you're balancing work with falling in love with your little sister's best friend and her daughter," he countered with a hint of humor.

I let my head fall forward, knowing I was busted. I turned around and looked at my best friend.

"I wasn't trying to fall in love with her. It kinda just happened."

"I know. It happens to the best of us. But I'm seriously happy for you. Maybe after things settle down after the holidays, we can all do dinner, and I can get to know them."

"I would like that, and I'm sure Avery would too."

I didn't want to talk about how I didn't know what the future held or if she would even still be here after the New Year. I finished his drink and then cleaned up the mess while he sneakily tried to pay for it. I grabbed the twenty he left and shoved it back in his hand as we walked out and locked up for the second time.

"I'm still doing Christmas dinner at the bar if you want to join us," Aiden said. "Avery and Kennedy are more than welcome as well."

"I'll talk to her and let you know," I replied, swallowing the ball of emotion sitting in my throat. "Have fun tonight. Be sure to have Jackie record it if you get wasted and decide to sing Celine Dion again."

"Not in your lifetime," he snorted. "I don't sing anymore, and no amount of liquor will get me to start again."

I shook my head and laughed as I climbed into my truck and headed home.

Twenty-Nine
Avery

"Do you need help?" I asked as Kennedy stood at the sink on a step stool and washed the veggies for the salad we were making for dinner.

"I got it, Momma."

I grinned and checked on the pasta that was boiling on the stove before peeking into the oven to make sure the chicken and garlic bread weren't burning.

I hadn't cooked a meal like this in so long I was doubting my ability to make something edible. Sam had been cooking for us so much lately that I wanted to return the favor. We were initially supposed to go to his parent's house for Sunday dinner, but they needed a little more time to finish their Christmas shopping.

Sam had texted a few minutes ago, saying he was on his way. I had hoped to have dinner ready before he walked in, but time wasn't on my side tonight. I heard the garage door open and then close before the door leading into the house opened.

"Uncle Sam!" Kennedy squealed, abandoning her veggies in the sink and running to him.

"Hey, Kennedy! How's my favorite girl doing?" He set his

stuff down on the closest table and picked her up, swinging her as she hugged him tightly.

"I'm good. I'm helping Mommy make dinner."

"Well, it smells delicious. What can I help with?"

"Do you want to make the salad?" she offered, leading him by the hand to the veggies she'd left in the sink.

"Sure. I can do that. But let me say hi to your mom first."

I smiled as he pulled me in for a hug and placed a kiss on my neck, where Kennedy couldn't see it. She knew we were dating, but we still tried our best to keep PDAs to a minimum when she was around. It wasn't like she was used to seeing her dad and I be affectionate with each other.

"Hi, welcome home," I said, already feeling flustered by his kiss.

"Thank you. I'm happy to be home," he replied, still standing close enough to keep the butterflies going in my stomach.

"Sam!" Kennedy called, interrupting us. "We have to make salad. It's healthy for you."

He stepped back and chuckled, looking down at my daughter, who was standing beside us.

"You can kiss mommy later, but right now, we make the salad." She grabbed his hand and pulled him over to the sink as she climbed back up on the step stool.

"Do you know how to cut with a knife?" she asked, sounding a little bossier than I liked.

"I do."

"Okay. I'll wash. You cut."

"Deal."

I grinned and let them be as I finished the rest of dinner and set the table.

Kennedy clapped excitedly as Sam set the salad bowl on the table beside the basket of bread and the chicken fettuccini alfredo I'd thrown together. She smiled as he helped her with the salad tongs before letting her serve herself.

My heart ached in the best way as I watched him with her, falling perfectly into the role of being a father figure without trying. I knew better than to allow my heart to fall any deeper than I had already, but I couldn't help myself.

We laughed and talked about our day while Kennedy and Sam had a contest to see who could chew their noodles the fastest as it hung from their mouth. They were silly, and dinner was lighthearted and fun, something I hadn't realized how much I had missed until now.

My phone dinged on the table with a new email alert that I would have typically ignored, but when I saw the subject line and sender, I rushed to open it.

"No phones at the dinner table, Mommy," Kennedy whined, likely more upset that I wasn't paying attention to their noodle contest than with me being on my phone.

"I'm sorry, honey," I said absently, my eyes quickly scanning the email message.

"What's wrong?" Sam asked, touching my hand to get my attention.

"A job I applied for in Houston wants to do a phone interview tomorrow. They're looking to quickly fill a spot for a second-grade teaching position at their school. If selected, I would start January 5th."

Sam sank back in his chair as his face fell.

Thirty

Sam

"I swear, I've never seen you so bah humbug before in all the years I've worked with you, and definitely never on Christmas Eve," Piper noted as we got everything ready to open for the day.

"I'm fine," I lied, trying to shake off my bad mood so I didn't ruin anyone else's.

I hadn't been able to stop thinking about how well Avery's interview had gone and how she'd been offered a teaching job in Houston. She was so excited about it, and I wanted to be happy for her, but how could I be when it meant she would be leaving? We spent the past few days doing stuff with Kennedy to get her excited about Christmas, which was also an excellent way for us to avoid dealing with the elephant in the room.

I knew that Avery didn't owe me anything and that we both went into whatever this was between us, knowing that it would be short-lived because she was never planning to stay. But deep down in my heart, I had hoped that confessing our love for one another would be enough to change her mind. I knew as a mother that she wanted to offer her daughter the best the world could give her, but I hated that. I felt like she was easily overlooking the fact that she could do that in Sugarplum Falls.

"You're the worst liar," Piper continued, restocking the disposable cups. Today would be a busy morning, with everyone stopping in to get their caffeine fix before the final countdown to make the magic happen.

"I'm not lying. I'm fine."

"Do I need to call Cassidy and ask her what's going on?"

"Not like she doesn't know. Avery *is* her best friend," I muttered.

I closed my eyes and sighed heavily when I realized I'd just spilled the beans.

"I knew it was Avery-related, but I haven't been able to figure out what."

"She got offered a teaching job in Houston, and I think she's going to take it. They want her to start right away, after New Year's. She told them she needed a few days and would let them know on the 26th."

"Oh. Shit." Piper's face fell along with her shoulders as she stopped what she was doing and looked at me. "I'm sorry, Sam. I know how much you like her."

"Not like. Love."

Piper's eyes widened as her hands went to her mouth.

"You're in love?"

I nodded and looked away, not wanting to feel so vulnerable right now.

"Sam, that's wonderful!"

"I think you're missing the whole point here, Piper," I

teased sarcastically. "It doesn't matter if I'm in love if the person I'm in love with wants to move to another state."

"Love isn't meant to be easy, Sam. You know that."

"Actually, I don't. I've never been in love until now. I thought I was before, but nothing has ever felt like this. None of the women I've dated have ever compared to Avery. While those relationships were good and I had a decent heartbreak after they ended, it will be nothing like what I will feel when Avery leaves me. It's not something I'll ever come back from."

"Who said it has to end?"

"You can't tell me that you think a long-distance relationship is the answer here?" I questioned with an arched eyebrow.

"Long-distance could be better than nothing. If you love her like you say you do, why not make every effort to be with her?"

"I don't know," I said with a sigh, knowing full well what the answer was.

"Stop lying."

I rolled my eyes and grabbed the towel to wipe down the counters again.

"It's not that easy, okay?"

"Why not? You love her. She loves you. You love each other. What am I missing here?"

"That clearly she and I are not on the same page," I nearly shouted, my emotions getting the best of me. "I love her so much, Piper. She and Kennedy mean more to me than anything in the world. But she didn't even bat an eye or consider staying here. Once she found out about the job offer in Houston, she was excited and more focused on taking the job. Never once did she stop and ask how I felt about it or if I would even be interested in trying to do a long-distance relationship."

"Oh. I see. It makes sense now." Piper pulled her mouth into a straight line and lowered her head.

"You see what?"

"Your real fear isn't that she's leaving, Sam. It's that she doesn't love you as much as you love her. You're angry because you fell hard for her without knowing if she felt the same way."

"She said she loved me," I countered, not wanting to admit that she was right.

"Yes, but deep down, you're wondering if it's enough."

She was right. I hadn't been able to stop thinking about how I loved Avery so much that I would do anything for her, including moving to Houston. But she never asked. She never once mentioned my name or how I would play into their new life once they moved. I wasn't just losing her; I was losing the little girl I had come to love as my own.

Thirty-One
Avery

"I think this is a terrible idea," I muttered to Cassidy as she continued on with her latest idea. "He is already pissed at me, Cass. He's hardly talked to me ever since I told him about the job in Houston."

"I know, but he will get over it."

"It's not that easy. I hurt him. I haven't even had a chance to tell him that I declined the job. For all I know, he's so mad at me that he won't even care if I stay in Sugarplum Falls. He'll probably call the school in Houston and demand that they take me so he can be done with me."

"You're being a bit dramatic."

"Says the girl who is measuring ribbon to tie around the box she wants her best friend to hide in."

"Hey—this is a brilliant idea. You guys have been fighting over the job in Houston so what better way to give him the news that you're going to stay in Sugarplum Falls than to make yourself into the best gift he has ever gotten?"

"Is mommy ready to get in the box?" Kennedy asked as she walked into the living room.

"Almost," Cassidy said. "But she needs to hurry up and get her butt in there before Sam gets home."

"Why does Sam want my mom as a Christmas gift?" Kennedy questioned, plopping down on the couch. Thankfully, we had more or less broken the habit of her calling him *Uncle Sam*.

"Umm…" Cassidy looked at me with a lost expression.

"Don't look at me. This was *your* crazy idea," I hissed so Kennedy couldn't hear me.

"Okay, enough out of you. Climb in the box, and I'll come wrap you up in a minute."

I rolled my eyes but carefully got in, making sure not to tear the cardboard in the process.

"Your mommy is getting in the box so she can surprise Sam when he gets home. She hasn't told him your guys' secret yet, so that's part of the gift she's giving him."

"Our secret?" Kennedy questioned, her eyebrows pulled together. "Is it that mommy is going to have a baby?!"

"No," I answered quickly, pinning Cassidy with a look before she could run with the idea again. It took me forever to convince her I wasn't pregnant the last time Kennedy said something. "Mommy is not having a baby. You're my only baby."

"But that's not fair," Kennedy grumbled, folding her arms over her chest and pouting.

"What's not fair, honey?" I asked, not having the energy to deal with this while trying not to fall out of the box.

"That Santa doesn't give me what I told him I wanted for Christmas."

"Oh, sweetheart. I'm sorry. I know that you want a baby sister or brother, but that's not something Santa can give you. That's something that happens between adults, and it's very complicated sometimes."

"The little girl in the movie got it," Kennedy countered, still upset about it.

I frowned for a moment, trying to recall which movie she was talking about. We watched so many recently that they were all starting to blur together.

"Miracle on 34th Street is a pretend movie," Cassidy explained, kneeling in front of her as she spoke softly. "While Santa is real, the movie wasn't. They were all actors and actresses."

"But it's not fair!" Kennedy cried louder, making my heart break.

Suddenly, we heard the garage door open, and Cassidy and I exchanged a panicked look.

"Here, take your sign," she said, grabbing it from the coffee table and throwing it at me as she jumped up. "Duck down, and I'll tape you up real quick."

"I can't believe I'm doing this," I hissed as I sat on the floor and let my eyes adjust to the darkness as Cassidy closed the top and taped it.

"Sam is coming, so we have to be quiet and not tell him that Mommy is in the box, okay?" Cassidy asked Kennedy. "I'll give you some of that fudge you like if you can sit with me on the couch and pretend we're watching TV."

"Cassidy!" I scolded, then immediately shut up as I heard

the door to the house opening at the same time the sound on the T.V. turned up.

"Hey, what are you doing here?" Sam asked, closing the door behind him.

"Oh, I'm just hanging out with Kennedy. Avery had to run a last-minute errand, so we're just chillin' and watching T.V. You know how much Kennedy likes her cartoons."

I didn't have to see the screen to know she was lying, given that a monotone man started talking about the recent snowfall and how Sugarplum Falls hadn't seen a storm like this in years. I closed my eyes and pressed the palm of my hand to my head.

"Umm, that's not cartoons. That's the news," Sam commented. "What's with the box?"

"Oh. Haha," Cassidy said, her voice going higher. "Silly me. I must've bumped the buttons and changed the channel on accident."

"You're being weird," Sam replied as he walked past, the sound of his footsteps getting closer to where I was hiding in the box.

"No way. I'm just being me," Cassidy nearly sang. She was about to lose it, and I was about to run out of air in this damn box.

"So, what's with the box? Do you need me to take it to Mom's for tomorrow?"

"Nope. That's actually for you. You can open it now."

"For me? How do you know? I don't see a name tag."

"It's from Avery. Open it," Cassidy pressed.

"Yeah, open it," Kennedy said, her mood already sounding happier.

"Shouldn't I wait for Avery to get back before I open it?"

"No. You should open it now while she's not here."

"Why? That doesn't make any sense. If it's from Avery, it's only fair that I wait until she's here to open it."

"She doesn't want to be here when you open it."

"Why not?"

"Ummm," Cassidy said nervously, and I could tell she was trying to pull something out of her ass at this point. We didn't have enough time to plan or think this through before committing to it. "She's mad at you."

My eyes bulged in the darkness of the box. I was going to kick her hard when I got out.

"What? Why is she mad at me?" Sam questioned, the hurt evident in his voice.

"You, of all people, should know why," Cassidy scoffed. "Now just open the damn gift."

"You said a bad word, Aunt Cassidy," Kennedy scolded.

"Sorry, sweetie. I'll give you two pieces of fudge to make up for it."

I rolled my eyes and shook my head. My kid was going to end up with cavities from all the sugar she was giving her these past few days.

"Hurry and open it," Cassidy pushed. "Avery will be back any minute now, and I promised her I would have you open it before she got here."

"Fine. But if she's mad about this, I'm blaming you," Sam warned as he pulled the piece of tape and started lifting the top flaps of the box.

I had planned to jump up and surprise him, but sitting in an awkward position had made my foot go to sleep.

"Surprise," I said awkwardly, holding up my sign for him to read.

"Avery?" he asked, looking past the sign I was using to hide my flushed face. "What are you doing in there?"

"Well, I was going to jump up and surprise you, but my foot fell asleep," I explained, realizing that my sign was backward so he couldn't see it.

"Okay, but why are you in a box to begin with?"

"I… umm…." I looked nervously at Cassidy, who was sitting on the couch, grinning wildly beside Kennedy.

"She's your gift, you dumbass," Cassidy blurted out.

"Another bad word," Kennedy pointed out, holding her hand out to Cassidy.

Cassidy reached into the box on the table, retrieved a piece of fudge, then handed it to Kennedy.

"You're going to pay for that," I said, pointing at Cassidy as I took the hand Sam extended to help me up.

"What does she mean that you're my gift?" he asked softly.

I lifted the sign for him to see and watched as his facial expressions changed as he read it.

"Ms. Harrison—Sugarplum Falls Elementary Kindergarten Teacher," he said, his eyes looking up to meet mine. "You're staying in Sugarplum Falls?"

I nodded, wiping an errant tear with the back of my hand.

"After I declined the position in Houston, Cassidy told me about a position that had just opened at Sugarplum Falls Elementary School. It's a kindergarten class, but I'm really excited about it."

Sam searched my face for a moment before looking at his sister to see if this was some sort of joke.

"Ms. Jackson decided to retire early. She told me about it the other day when she came into Waldon's. I immediately called Avery and told her to go to the school and see if they would let her interview for it. Everything just kinda fell into place after that," Cassidy explained.

"I can't believe you're staying," Sam whispered, holding the sign and continuing to stare at it.

I couldn't tell whether he was relieved or disappointed that we weren't going to Houston after all.

"Is that a good thing or…"

"It's a wonderful thing, Avery. It's the best present you could have ever given me."

"Well then, I guess I'll take the other stuff back," I teased, giggling when he reached down and tickled my sides.

"I don't need anything other than you and Kennedy. I can't

tell you how happy I am that you guys are staying. How will it work with you being the kindergarten teacher and her starting kindergarten next year?" he asked.

"I talked to the principal and explained everything. She said that she didn't see an issue with it and that we would make changes as needed. But since Sugarplum Falls is such a small town, they can't really do anything about it because there's only one elementary school and only one kindergarten teacher. But I gotta admit that I'm happy I'll get to experience her first year of school alongside her and that we get to stay in Sugarplum Falls. It turned out *you* were the sign I was looking for all along."

"That's amazing. I still can't believe the good news. I mean, I wish I would have been more prepared, but like my grandfather always used to say, sometimes good things happen when you least expect them." Sam shoved a hand through his hair nervously, then looked from Cassidy and Kennedy to me.

"I know that staying in Sugarplum Falls wasn't something you planned on doing, but I'm so glad you are. I hope that you and Kennedy will continue living with me because you've made my house into a home, and I wouldn't want it any other way. I have a question I'd like to ask you, but because I wasn't prepared for this, I'm going to have to wing a few things."

My heart began racing as he pulled two candy canes out of his back pocket and then dropped to one knee.

"Avery, you've shown me what true love is, and I can't imagine a life without you and Kennedy. You've already made me the happiest man in the world when you told me you loved me, but I would love it if you'd give me the honor of being my wife and making me the happiest man again. I don't have a ring because I wasn't planning to do this right now—"

"Sam, you don't have to—"

"No, Avery. I want to. I want to ask you to marry me more than I want anything else. And while I don't have a ring right this moment, I have these two candy canes," he said with a smile.

"Women want diamonds, dumbass. Not candy canes," Cassidy commented from the couch.

Sam glared at her before returning his focus to me.

"I'm probably a little crazy for doing this, but this feels right, Avery. And I will buy you all the diamonds in the world if that's what you want. But for now, I present to you the symbol of love that my grandfather used to always tell me about. When they're separate, they're just candy canes. But when you put them together, they make a heart. Without you, I'm just a guy who makes some of the best coffee in Sugarplum Falls. But with you, I'm the luckiest man in the world who still makes the best coffee."

I rolled my eyes and shook my head.

"And still so humble," I teased, whispering loudly behind my hand.

"Avery, will you accept my candy cane heart with the promise that I will get you a real engagement ring, and be my wife?"

I covered my mouth and nodded, the tears already filling my eyes.

"Yes, Sam. I'll marry you!"

He stood up and wrapped me in the tightest hug as Kennedy and Cassidy cheered for us from the couch.

178

Thirty-Two
Sam

I sat at the dinner table, grinning like a fool as Kennedy told us about the arts and crafts projects she did with my parents for Christmas. It felt surreal that not only were Avery and Kennedy staying in Sugarplum Falls but that Avery had agreed to marry me.

I felt bad for not having an actual ring, but she didn't seem to care. Her smile had been just as big as mine, and she refused to let go of my hand when she didn't have to. It was like she needed to touch me any way she could, and the feeling was mutual.

After dinner, we all sat down in the living room to open one present before bed. This was a tradition that my family had always done when I was growing up, and I made sure to ask Avery about it before suggesting it to Kennedy.

Not only was I about to have a wife, but I was also getting the most incredible daughter. I couldn't wait to start the process of officially adopting Kennedy, even though Avery and I agreed that it didn't matter how long it took because she was already mine. Plus, we had all the time in the world now that they weren't leaving.

"Which one should we have Sam open?" Avery asked Kennedy as they sat on the floor in front of the Christmas tree.

"This one!" Kennedy said, pointing to a small box sitting on top of a stack of larger ones that were for Kennedy.

"Are you sure?" Avery tilted her head and smiled.

"Yes!" Kennedy gently grabbed it from her mom and handed it to me.

"Here you go!"

"Thank you, Kennedy." I held the present to my chest while she giggled.

"Do you think you can help me pick one for your mom?" I asked, leaning around Avery to grab a few from the stack I had wrapped and put under the tree this morning.

"Sure!"

Kennedy looked through the different-sized boxes and then handed her mom a medium-sized one.

"Alright. Now that we all have one present, let's open them."

Kennedy immediately ripped the wrapping paper off of hers, squealing when she found a baby doll she had seen on TV.

"It's the baby!" she shrieked, grinning ear to ear as she cuddled it to her chest while checking out all of the accessories that went with it. Thankfully, Avery had already unpacked everything and put the batteries in. She leaned over and gently flipped the switch to turn it on so Kennedy could hear it cry.

"I love it so much! Thank you, Momma!"

"You're welcome, sweet girl. But it's from me and Sam."

"Thank you, Sam!"

Kennedy got up and wrapped her arms around my neck, squeezing tightly as she hugged me.

"You're welcome."

I hadn't helped Avery with that gift for Kennedy, but I knew that our lives were already starting to change, and she was taking the first step by including me in everything that involved her daughter. If that wasn't one of the greatest gifts of all, I didn't know what was.

"You next," I said, nodding to Avery, who was still holding her gift.

"How about we open them at the same time?" she suggested, smiling at me.

"Deal."

We both unwrapped our gifts, and I loved the small gasp that escaped her lips when she found the delicate gold heart necklace I had picked for her. I hadn't seen her wear much jewelry, but I had noticed the way she admired it when we went shopping.

"Oh my gosh, Sam! This is beautiful. Thank you so much!"

"You're welcome."

I opened the lid of the small box Kennedy had picked for me and slowly opened it. Inside was a clay ornament in the shape of Kennedy's hand. In the middle, she'd written my name in red paint with a heart underneath it.

"Kennedy, did you make this for me?" I asked, my throat tight with emotion. I held it up for her to see, making sure I didn't accidentally break it.

She nodded and grinned while setting her baby down to give it a bottle.

"Thank you so much. It's so beautiful."

"You're welcome," she replied as she picked the baby up and started to burp it. It seemed a bit fast for it to have finished eating, but what did I know about babies?

"Alright, my love. We've opened one gift for tonight, but now it's time to get to bed. Santa can't come if we're up playing all night," Avery said to Kennedy as she stood up and collected the few pieces of trash from our gifts.

"Okay, Momma. Can Sam sit with us while you read tonight?"

"Of course, he's more than welcome to if he'd like to," Avery said, giving me a nervous look.

"I would love to."

I wrapped my arms around Avery's waist while we waited for Kennedy to get up. This was just the beginning of the most wonderful life I could have ever imagined.

Thirty-Three

Avery

I woke up Christmas morning, snuggled against Sam as we heard Kennedy screeching from her room that it was Christmas morning.

"It's time to get up," I said with a soft laugh, patting his arm so he'd release me. "You have about two seconds before she—"

Before I could get my words out, Kennedy came flying into the room and jumped on the bed.

"It's Christmas! It's Christmas! Get up! We have to see if Santa came!"

She bounced excitedly as Sam groaned while taking a jab to his side from one of her bounces.

"Alright, sweetie. Give us a few minutes and we'll be right there. Go ahead and wait in your room, and we'll come get you."

"Okay, Mommy!"

She jumped off the bed and went running down the short hall back to her room.

It was weird staying in Sam's bed last night, but after we'd talked to Kennedy about the changes that were going to happen with Sam and I getting married, she seemed to be okay with everything. It could also be that she was just in a Christmas excited stupor and didn't process any of what we'd said.

"Are you okay?" I asked, worried she'd hurt him. At least it was on his side and not on his balls.

"Yeah. I'll live." He climbed out of bed and stretched his arms above his head, a sliver of abs teasing me in the process.

"Well, that's good because I didn't agree to marry you only to have you die before we have our wedding day," I teased, pulling on my robe. It wasn't chilly in the house I just really loved how comfy it was.

"Why does she have to wait to go in the living room?" Sam asked, following me down the hallway.

"Because she will be overcome with excitement and open everything before we get in there if not."

"Gotcha. Good to know."

I felt his hand on my lower back as we stopped at Kennedy's door. She was sitting on the floor in front of the pink Christmas tree Sam had given her, putting the star topper on. It had a beautiful assortment of ornaments on it from the advent calendar he'd given her.

"You ready?" I asked, a huge smile crossing my face.

"Yes!"

"Alright. You lead the way. Let's see if Santa stopped by last night."

Sam and I had stayed up a few hours after getting Kennedy to bed last night, initially to get the gift from Santa into the living room. That only took a few minutes, and then the rest of the time was spent with Sam pretending to be Santa and having me sit on his lap as I told him exactly what I wanted.

We walked into the living room and Sam turned on the lights right as Kennedy stepped inside. Sitting in front of the tree was the large box with the dollhouse from Santa.

I leaned forward and grinned when I saw how big her eyes and smile were.

"Is that from Santa?" she asked, her voice barely above a whisper.

"There's only one way to find out," I said, gently giving her a push forward.

She rushed over to the box and immediately looked for the name tag, even though she couldn't read much of it. We were practicing, but she would definitely learn more once she started kindergarten, and we could focus on it daily.

"What does it say?" she asked, looking up at me. "It has different wrapping paper, so it has to be from Santa, right?"

I grinned, loving how Sam had had the idea to wrap it in a different wrapping paper than any of the other gifts. He insisted that anything from Santa needed that specific wrapping paper, then we would hide what was left so she didn't see it.

"It says *to Kennedy from Santa*," I said, pointing to each word.

"Oh my gosh!" She covered her mouth with her hands and looked from the present to me, then back to the box.

"Well, go on and open it!" I encouraged as Sam sat in the recliner and recorded her on his phone.

I helped her as needed, tossing the box to the side once the dollhouse was fully unwrapped. She squealed and jumped up and down excitedly as she thanked Santa over and over. Her happiness made my heart full.

We moved the dollhouse to the side so we could continue opening presents, though we had to promise her that she'd have plenty of time to play with it before we went to lunch at Sam's parent's house. It was a busy day, and I felt a bit nervous to go to dinner with him tonight because it was at his friend's bar, and I hadn't had the time to really get to know anyone yet. Cassidy had asked if she could keep Kennedy for a few hours tonight while we went, and I knew it was more for Sam and me to have some alone time on Christmas than anything. But I appreciated it nonetheless.

The gifts were opened in record time, both Sam and I smiling the whole time as Kennedy continued to freak out over how amazing her presents were. Sam had gotten some stuff we hadn't talked about, but I couldn't be mad at how much he loved my daughter. This was just the beginning of a life filled with more love and happiness than I could have ever imagined.

****

Ready for more steamy holiday goodness? Be sure to check out these spicy novellas as well! And if you'd like to chat books, be sure to find me in my reader group!

Samantha Baca's Smutties

https://www.facebook.com/groups/2945710968775398/

Blame It On The Mistletoe
https://books2read.com/u/bw1rqe

Blame It On The Eggnog
https://books2read.com/u/38PPY6

Blame It On The Candy Canes
https://books2read.com/u/31DNo7

<u>Other Books By Samantha Baca</u>

<u>The Haven Brook Series</u>
<u>(small-town romantic suspense):</u>

'Til Death Do Us Part (Haven Brook Book 1)

https://books2read.com/u/m2RJNR

The Cradle Will Fall (Haven Brook Book 2)

https://books2read.com/u/b6O0QE

The Ties That Bind (Haven Brook Book 3)

https://books2read.com/u/mqgoz8

A Very Haven Christmas (Haven Brook Book 4- Novella)

https://books2read.com/u/mvqGjj

Three Strikes, You're Gone (Haven Brook Book 5)

https://books2read.com/u/mvqL2z

<u>The Dark Shadows Trilogy</u>
<u>(romantic suspense)</u>

Five Steps Ahead (Dark Shadows Book 1)

https://books2read.com/u/38Q0gO

Ten Seconds Too Late (Dark Shadows Book 2)

https://books2read.com/u/3JRgVB

Against The Clock (Dark Shadows Book 3)

https://books2read.com/u/m2YwoR

<u>The Stone Creek Series</u>
<u>(small-town- novellas)</u>

Chocolate Covered Mistletoe (Stone Creek Book 1)

https://books2read.com/u/3LRk9N

Candy Coated Promises (Stone Creek Book 2)

https://books2read.com/u/mldP5Y

Pumpkin Spiced Possibilities (Stone Creek Book 3)

https://books2read.com/u/bojdwV

Beaumont Creek Series (small town)

Just One Time (Beaumont Creek Book 1)

https://books2read.com/u/3G52zK

Second Chances (Beaumont Creek Book 2)

https://books2read.com/u/4Aj6Z0

Third Time's The Charm (Beaumont Creek Book 3)

https://books2read.com/u/b5lEyG

Four-ever Single (Beaumont Creek Book 4)

https://books2read.com/u/4j5jMX

Fifth Wheel (Beaumont Creek Book 5)

https://books2read.com/u/4XwKwa

<u>Whiskey Mountain Series</u>
<u>(small-town- novellas)</u>

Something To Talk About

https://books2read.com/u/4X62ag

Something To Think About

https://books2read.com/u/3GWAan

Something To Believe In

https://books2read.com/u/3yVzgB

Something To Live For

https://books2read.com/u/mllEOP

<u>Sugarplum Falls Series</u>
<u>(Holiday Novellas- can be read as standalone)</u>

Blame It On The Mistletoe
https://books2read.com/u/bw1rqe

Blame It On The Eggnog
https://books2read.com/u/38PPY6

Blame It On The Candy Canes
https://books2read.com/u/31DNo7

Blame It On The Blizzard
https://books2read.com/u/b6z6XE

Blame It On The Reindeer
https://books2read.com/u/baLAG6

Blame It On The Carols
https://books2read.com/u/me8E9z

Blame It On The Lattes
https://books2read.com/u/mB1E2A

Blame It On The Secret Santa
https://books2read.com/u/mY9dGY

<u>Standalone Books</u>

One Last Wish

https://books2read.com/u/mqg7D9

Finding Love In Apartment 2C (novella)

https://books2read.com/u/bze9aZ

Cocky Counsel: A Hero Club Novel

https://books2read.com/u/31Kzkn

All Is Fair In Food And War (novella)

https://books2read.com/u/bp8qjX

<u>Holiday Books (novellas)</u>

Snow Place To Go

https://books2read.com/u/4A560N

A Very Merry Kissmas

https://books2read.com/u/bPDgy7

A Christmas Wish

https://books2read.com/u/4EKXpE

Holiday Hijinks

https://books2read.com/u/4DP6Ze

<u>Acknowledgments</u>

Thank you to all of the wonderful people who made this book possible. My alpha readers—Amanda, Claire, Valerie, and Azucena—you ladies do an incredible job of keeping me on track and making the story better! My beta readers—Malissa, Jackie, Tamara, and Karrie—I couldn't do this without you! I appreciate the quick feedback and all of the little things you find that we missed in the first few hundred rounds of looking over this book! Okay, that might be a little dramatic, but sometimes it feels like it's been that many!

As always, I wouldn't be where I am without my wonderful, incredible readers. Whether you've ARC read this for me or you grabbed your copy to read on release day—I appreciate and value you so much! Thank you for your support!

My family will always be my biggest and loudest supporters! Thank you all for loving me unconditionally as I continue to chase my dreams. I love you so much!

We all know how much my wonderful husband, Richard, supports me. Without his help, there's a lot I wouldn't get done. Thank you for always stepping in to help with covers and formatting and talking me off the ledge when I need it. I will always be indebted to you. I love you!

My sweet girls. 30+ books later, and I still believe that you can have the world as long as you try. Don't ever worry about goals being too big or too hard. If I can do it, you most certainly can. I love you both more than you'll ever know!

If you enjoyed this book and would love to tell your fellow book lovers all about it, please consider leaving a review on any retailer of your choice! It's always greatly appreciated!

You can find them here:

https://books2read.com/u/mB1E2A

About the Author

Samantha lives in the southwest with her husband and two small children after abandoning her childhood dream of living in a cabin in Colorado when she found that she couldn't afford to live there and was deathly allergic to the woods. When she's not writing, she's usually spouting off sarcastic remarks while drinking wine out of a coffee mug to look like a functional adult while chasing down her toddlers. She enjoys spending time with her family, watching reruns of Friends, and the 24/7 flow of coffee that can be found in her veins. Be sure to follow her on social media for updates on what she's working on.

You can find her here:

Facebook:

https://www.facebook.com/AuthorSamanthaBaca

Instagram: https://instagram.com/author_samantha_baca

Goodreads: http://www.goodreads.com/authorsamanthabaca

Facebook Reader Group: https://www.facebook.com/groups/2945710968775398/

Webpage: www.samanthabaca.com

Newsletter: http://eepurl.com/g0NcSj